the gate

"Dann Stouten is a master storyteller. There is a real world all around us. We taste and feel it every day. There is also another world where God dwells and those who have gone before us live with Jesus. Dann Stouten helps us discover that these two places intersect more than we often notice. If we pay close attention, we just might see, smell, and learn to taste the goodness of a world beyond this one. Here is my advice: get this book, pour a cup of coffee, find a comfortable chair, and enjoy!"

—**Kevin Harney**, lead pastor of Shoreline Church in Monterey, CA, and author of *Reckless Faith* and the Organic Outreach series

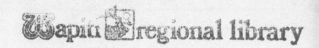
the gate

A NOVEL

DANN A. STOUTEN

Revell

a division of Baker Publishing Group
Grand Rapids, Michigan

Published by Revell
a division of Baker Publishing Group
P.O. Box 6287, Grand Rapids, MI 49516-6287
www.revellbooks.com

Printed in the United States of America

Library of Congress Cataloging-in-Publication Data
Stouten, Dann A., 1949–
    The Gate : a novel / Dann A. Stouten.
        pages cm
    ISBN 978-0-8007-2109-1 (pbk.)
    1. Christian fiction. I. Title.
PS3619.T6976G38   2013
813′.6—dc23   2012043700

Most Scripture used in this book, whether quoted or paraphrased by the characters, is taken from the Holy Bible, New International Version®. NIV®. Copyright © 1973, 1978, 1984, 2011 by Biblica, Inc.™ Used by permission of Zondervan. All rights reserved worldwide. www.zondervan.com

Some Scripture quotations are taken from The Holy Bible, English Standard Version® (ESV®), copyright © 2001 by Crossway, a publishing ministry of Good News Publishers. Used by permission. All rights reserved. ESV Text Edition: 2007

The internet addresses, email addresses, and phone numbers in this book are accurate at the time of publication. They are provided as a resource. Baker Publishing Group does not endorse them or vouch for their content or permanence.

13   14   15   16   17   18   19   7   6   5   4   3   2   1

Dedicated to the people I love, the people I've lost, and the God who's promised to prepare a place where all of us can spend eternity together with him.

Acknowledgments

I want to thank Kevin Harney for being my friend, for believing in my writing, and for badgering people in the publishing world into giving the book a second look.

I want to thank Vicki Crumpton for taking my rambling stories and turning them into a book. Her skill as an editor and her passion to make this book better have made all the difference.

I want to thank everyone at Baker Publishing Group and the Revell division for investing in me and my writing.

I want to thank the congregation of Community Reformed Church for their partnership in the gospel all these years and for their willingness to listen to my stories.

And finally I thank God for his grace, for my family, and for the way that each has shaped my life. Words fail to express my gratitude.

lost

Not all those who wander are lost;

The old that is strong does not wither,

Deep roots are not reached by the frost.

J. R. R. Tolkien,
The Lord of the Rings

1

The ad on the internet intrigued me. I'd been looking at cabins and cottages when the picture of an old inn caught my eye. I couldn't be sure, since it had been over forty years since I'd been there, but for the life of me, it looked like the cottage my family rented every July when I was a kid. The ad said that it was being used as a supper club. It claimed that the food and the view were heavenly and that it could be booked by the week or purchased outright. For a few minutes I studied the pictures in the ad and let my mind play with the possibilities.

Across the front of a huge screened-in porch were fieldstone columns, spaced about four feet apart, lined up like soldiers. The outside was covered in white lap siding with moss green–colored wood shingles tucked inside each of the peaks and the portico. The window trim and doors were painted in a darker green accented with red trim, and from the pictures, it looked to be well maintained and ready for occupancy.

The property was listed by a guy named Michael DeAngelo from Paradise Realty. The ad said, "Angel's Gate—the back door to God's country," and I noticed there was an open house scheduled for the weekend.

I showed the ad to Carol and said that this was the kind of place our grandkids would want to come and visit. We didn't have any grandkids yet, but I wanted to be prepared.

"You know I've given this some serious thought," I said. "And I've decided that I want to be the fun grandpa. I want to take them fishing and teach them how to swim, and sail, and roast marshmallows on a stick. And having a cottage would help in that department."

"Maybe you should go check it out on Friday when the girls and I go shopping in Chicago," Carol said. "You've got the week off anyway."

I had scheduled a week of vacation so that Carol and I could get away for a few days. I'd been under a lot of stress at work, and I needed a break. But when our daughter Kelly heard we were going shopping in Chicago, she thought it sounded like fun, so Carol invited her to go along. Then a few days later, Carol talked to our two other daughters, Tara and Kate, and somewhere along the line, Chicago became an all-girl getaway, and I got the boot.

They thought my Outback would be better for carrying packages, so they left me with Carol's Volkswagen. It was kind of girly—robin's egg blue with a dove gray convertible top. I pretended to be embarrassed to drive it, but to be honest, I was just as happy. It had been a while since I'd been up north, and I was going to put the top down and get a little sunshine.

The idea of spending a little time alone sounded pretty good to me. I'd been burning the candle at both ends for too long, and a few days with nothing to do and no one to worry about sounded like heaven.

I'd lost a lot of people I loved in the last year, and death has a way of layering up on you. It has this cumulative effect. It's like putting rocks in your knapsack. You hardly notice the first one, but the more you add, the more it starts to weigh you down. You still might be able to hobble your way along, but the people who care about you can't help but notice that something's wrong.

That's where I was. Carol kept asking me if I was all right, and I kept saying, "Sure, I'm fine. I'm just tired." But we both knew better.

Especially with what happened earlier that week.

It was a Tuesday, about ten in the morning, and I didn't see it coming. My cell phone rang, and the voice on the other end of the line said, "We've got a problem, bro!"

I recognized the voice, and the words were ones I'd heard many times before. It was my brother, Ben. He had a knack for getting into trouble, and I was the first one he called every time "we" had a problem. Today was no exception.

The two of us owned a used car lot together, but there had come a point in my life when I felt like God was pressing me toward something else. I'd dropped out of college during my senior year when I saw the chance to make some real money in the car business. It was a decision I'd always regretted, so finally after ten years I went back to school. It took me about a year to get my undergraduate degree, and during that time I continued to work with Ben at the lot. When I entered the doctor of psychology program at State, Ben sort of took over the business, and he'd been running it ever since. I still went to the auction once in a while, and I tried to cover Ben when he went on vacation, but Europa Motors was his baby now. For the most part, Ben ran a clean house, and there were certain lines I wouldn't let him cross, but he had a habit of sticking his toe over the line when I wasn't looking. This was one of those times, and I hadn't been looking.

We owned the lot, but Old State Bank owned the cars. They gave us a line of credit called a "floor plan," and our limit was 250 thousand. That limit was one of those lines that Ben liked to cross, but usually he was able to sell a car or two before the bank realized we were over. The bank knew it happened, but as long as it didn't get out of hand, they'd usually look the other way. The vice president in charge of the auto group was Jake Vander Molen. He'd been with Old State for thirty years, and even when things got a little hairy, I could usually talk him off the edge.

"You've got to call Jake," Ben said, "and tell him to get that new checker off my back. I'm doing the best I can. It ain't like there are a lot of buyers out there. The market's soft. It's been soft for over a year. They're just going to have to float it for a while."

"Calm down," I said. "Tell me what's going on, and I'll see what I can do."

"Like I said, they got this new checker. Said his name was Larry. He's nothing but a kid in a suit, and he was playing hardball with me. He said he'd jerk our floor plan if we'd didn't get things under the line by next Friday."

"Okay," I replied. "So sell something. Wholesale something if you have to."

"Don't go all big brother on me! We're in a little deeper than that. Our cash flow has been running downhill for a while now, and you're blind if you didn't see that. And, well, I did what I had to do. I sold a car or two and used the money to pay some bills, and I guess I didn't pay off the bank."

"A car or two?" I asked. "The bank doesn't usually get that upset about a car or two."

"Okay, it was seven cars and a pickup, but I always intended to pay them off. I just needed a little time. We always get caught up, but when I told this Larry that we were good for it, he said, 'God may give you grace, but not Old State.' I'm telling you, that kid was a whisper away from me smacking him. I wanted to take him out back and teach him some manners."

"Like that would do a lot of good," I said.

"Sky, if you'd have been here, you'd have felt the same way. You've got to call Jake and fix this."

When Ben was little, my given name, Schuyler, was too much of a mouthful, so he shortened it to Sky. Now that's what most everyone calls me.

I hung up and called Jake, but the news was worse than I thought.

"Listen, Sky," Jake said. "You know I've always liked you and your brother. We go way back, and your old man was always straight with me too, but my job's on the line with this one. The home office sent Larry out here to clean up some of the paper. The bank got hurt in the mortgage meltdown, and now they're dotting the i's and crossing the t's on everything, including floor plans. I pulled a loan on the sticks in your office for twenty, shuffled a few things around, buried a couple bills due from the Chicago Auction, and ignored a couple more from Grand Rapids, but that's only going to buy you a month or so."

"You put my office furniture up as collateral without talking to me?" I asked.

"It was that or shut you down, so you better just thank me and then get down here and sign the loan."

"Why didn't you take the loan out against the lot?" I asked. After we paid off our loan years ago, we signed up for a line of credit using the lot as collateral for exactly this sort of thing.

"Your brother took a major loan on the lot last year, and property values have dropped some since then. You know that. You co-signed, remember?"

"Oh, I guess so," I said, knowing that Ben must have signed it for me. Like I said, he had a habit of sticking his toe over the line. "So tell me, Jake, how bad are things looking?"

"It's pretty bad, Sky," Jake answered. "Your little brother's been upside-down since he and Mary Alice got divorced. Why he let her have the house and all I'll never know."

"You know Ben," I replied. "If Mary Alice mentioned their kid, he melted like a snowman in August. There's probably more to it than that, but that's what I know. Anyway, I'll get a handle on things and get back with you, and I'll get down there tomorrow to sign that note. And Jake . . . thanks. I appreciate you covering for us."

I drove over to the car lot to find Ben sitting with his feet up on the desk talking to Donny. Donny was our lot boy. Ben always said that if Donny was a girl he'd marry him. He never questioned anything you said, never gave you any back talk, and did whatever you told him to do.

Donny was thirty-six, and to put it gently, he was slow. He was a wiry little man with slicked-back, jet-black hair. He had on his typical costume: blue jeans cuffed up too high, red high-top Michael Jordans, and a white T-shirt with our logo on it. Chest high, the T-shirt said "Europa Motors" in bold, black block letters that were set in a multicolored band of international flags that ran all around the shirt.

"Hello, Mr. Sky," Donny said.

"Hey, Donny! Would you take this ten-spot and run over to the 7-Eleven and get us all a Coke?"

"And E-Z too?" he asked. E-Z was Ezekiel, Ben's boy, who was out in the wash bay waxing a black Audi A6. We called him "Easy," but with Donny's southern drawl, it came out "E-Z."

"Of course, get Easy one too, and a candy bar if he wants."

When Donny was out of earshot, Ben looked at me with his head tilted, flicked his longish dishwater-blond hair out of his eyes, and asked, "You don't like him much, do you, bro?"

"Listen," I said. "This isn't about Donny and you know it. I called the bank to clean up your mess, and I found out you took out a loan and signed my name on it."

Ben looked like he'd been pulled through a knot hole. There were dark circles under his eyes, he hadn't shaved, and his gray stubble made him look like an older Sonny Crockett from *Miami Vice*. He was wearing a crisp, yellow madras plaid shirt with a polo player on the pocket, khaki pants, no socks, and blue Docksides. For the first time ever, I noticed that my younger brother was getting old. He took a long, deep breath, and for a minute he looked down at the floor and slowly shook his head. Then he looked up at me with stern, steely gray eyes and squinted like Clint Eastwood in those old spaghetti westerns.

"It had to be done," he began, "and you weren't around to do it. It was when you were in Florida last year, and I didn't want to spoil your vacation. I meant to talk to you about it, but something always came up. First Mom died, then Grandma Great Kate, and then Mary Alice and I separated, and I guess I haven't had my mind on business much."

"Well, you better get your head in the game, or you'll be selling sporting goods at Walmart."

"Are you threatening me, bro?"

"No, I'm not threatening you, I'm telling you how it is! If I didn't back your play down at the bank, you'd be going to jail tomorrow instead of going to the auction."

Just then Donny and Easy came in with the Cokes, and even though there was a lot left unsaid, we let it slide.

Easy asked if there was anything good on the presale sheet for tomorrow's auction, and Ben said he had his eye on a few cars, but for sure he had to get the casket gray Tribeca for a customer from up north.

Ben took a deposit on the car on an "if," which is to say he had it sold if he could find a car that fit the customer's parameters. The Tribeca was close, so he was going to bid it to the nines. Of course, when he described the car to the customer, he told him the color was old world pewter. It worked that way with every color. If we were selling it, it was executive silver, but if somebody was trying to sell it to us or trade it in, then it was garbage can gray. Ben was a master at coming up with these names. Black was midnight pearl if we were selling it and a tar pit dust magnet if we were buying it.

"The old man could sell ice cubes to Eskimos," Easy said with a grin.

Looking at him, I couldn't help but think that Easy was looking more and more like Ben did before the accident. He was tall and handsome, with long, blond, curly hair, a muscular build, and a mischievous smile. Easy was going to be a sophomore this fall, and already the girls were falling all over him. Like his dad and his grandfather, he was a natural athlete. He was the starting guard on the Indians varsity basketball team, and he could pull up and hit the three anytime. On the basketball floor he'd earned the name "Big Easy," and even now, everybody knew he had a scholarship in his future. Easy wanted to play football, but Ben had talked him into golf.

"It's something you can do the rest of your life," Ben had maintained. "Sports are great. They'll teach you about teamwork and winning and losing, and you need that, but they don't last." It was the same reason Ben wanted Easy to play tennis in the spring.

"How long until you turn sixteen, Easy?" I asked.

"'Bout three months."

"Just think," I said, "then you'll be able to drive . . . legally."

We all laughed. Easy had been driving cars around the lot since he was ten, and for the last few years, Ben would send Easy and Donny if he needed a runner to pick something up at the auction or the body shop. Donny said they were a team, and he even had a name for them. He said they were "Slow and Easy," and after a while, the name stuck.

We sat and talked for a while, and then Donny and Easy went back out to the shop.

"Listen, Ben," I said. "You have to sell some cars, that's a given. But turning a few car deals isn't going to be enough and you know it. I've bought you a little time here, but that's all I'm going to do. The ball's in your court now. I don't know what you're going to do, but you'd better do something. I'm not bailing you out again even if it means we lose this place. I'm as serious as a heart attack about this, little brother. Somehow you've got to inject some cash into this place. To be honest with you, short of a miracle, I don't see how you're going to do it, so if I were you I'd start praying, and I'm not kidding."

As I walked out the door Ben said, "Don't worry, bro—Slow and Easy and I'll get it done. And as for the praying, I'll get that done too. I've already been talking to God about this. We just need a little time to work things out, that's all."

———

I needed a little time too, a little time away from all this. I looked at several cottages, but my mind kept coming back to the old inn. Why was I so intrigued by this place? Was it really the same place that had pinned so many warm memories to the soft places of my heart? Would such a place do the same thing for my children and grandchildren? Curiosity and nostalgia beat my thoughts back and forth like a tennis ball until I finally gave in.

"Maybe you're right," I said to Carol. "While you're gone, I think I'm going to take a drive up there and check it out. It's a short drive, only a few hours."

"You should!" Carol replied with that little grin that said she didn't believe me.

"I'm serious!" I insisted, and the conversation ended.

That was Tuesday night, and by Friday I was sure she'd forgotten all about it. I loaded her luggage in the car, kissed her good-bye, and went back inside, and there on my dresser was the ad for the inn with the directions to get there.

Did Carol do that? I wondered. *Or did I inadvertently hit* PRINT *the other night?*

I couldn't be sure. Either way, the idea was growing on me, and after lunch, I started meandering my way up north.

I stopped in North Bay and got lost in Barnes & Noble for part of the afternoon, and then I went out to the state park and took a long walk on the beach. There's something soothing about the rhythmic melody of waves slapping against the shore, and as I walked, I also began to unwind. Little kids were building sand castles, and an old woman in a big straw hat dozed in a lawn chair.

It was about six thirty when I got a couple of Coney dogs at the Dog 'n Suds. I walked out on the pier and watched the sunset as I ate my supper. An old man in a pair of tattered bib overalls and a T-shirt had a couple of nice perch in a bucket, and he and I struck up a conversation about the weather.

"It was a gorgeous day," he said. "But with the wind kicking up like that and those dark clouds rolling in, it's a sure sign of rain."

He began reeling in his line and picking up his gear, and I slurped down the last mouthful of my root beer float and made my way to the car.

I got back in the Beetle as lightning flashed across the darkening sky. I pushed the button to put the top up and started driving north again. I had intended to stay at a little hotel about a block from the highway, but as I pulled off the exit, I noticed that the neon sign said "No Vacancy." I could backtrack about twenty miles to the Holiday Inn in North Bay, turn around and take my curiosity home with me, or try to find Angel's Gate before dark. I chose the latter.

I made my way north along Oceania Drive, then I turned down Old Mill Road and began looking for the little two-track road that led back to the cottage. The pitter-patter of raindrops on the roof and the swish-slosh of the wipers lulled me along.

A lot had changed since I was a boy, but I'd occasionally recognize an old landmark. The building for the Chuck Wagon Restaurant where we'd get greasy burgers and strawberry malts was still there, but it was a laundromat now. The big rock and the flagpole still stood like sentinels outside the general store, and the baseball park with the broken backstop was still across the street. The road turned from blacktop to gravel just past the old iron bridge, and I knew I was getting close.

About three miles down the gravel road, I passed a row of mailboxes and turned down a two-track road that ran next to the old cemetery. There were two red brick columns on either side of the drive joined by an arch. Tucked in the weeds to the right of the drive was a Paradise Realty sign, and I was confident that I'd found Angel's Gate. The road ran parallel to a low brick wall capped with concrete that had a black wrought-iron fence on top. The little two-track path was not well-traveled, and I crept along carefully, expecting to see the old cottage at any minute.

The rain had intensified, the road was in worse shape than I expected, and before I got ten yards in, I splashed through a huge puddle and found myself up to the running boards in mud. I was stuck and unable to move. If I had been in my Outback, this would just be a momentary inconvenience. With its all-wheel drive, I'd bounce right through this, but in Carol's Bug, I knew I was in trouble. I tried my best to rock the car loose, but it was no use. The mud was a foot deep and as slippery as a wet goldfish.

I thought about calling for a tow truck, but there were no signal bars on my cell phone. I tried again to rock the car loose, but I was stuck like a Dutchman with his finger in the dike. I finally turned off the ignition and watched the headlights slowly fade to black. I was hoping to see a light or some sign of life, but no. There was nothing I could do but wait until morning, so I cranked the seat back and closed my eyes, and eventually the rhythmic drumming of the rain drowned out my frustration and lulled me to sleep.

It had been a long time since I'd spent the night in a car, and in the morning my foot was asleep, my back was stiff, and my mouth tasted like night crawlers. I had only two choices: I could go back the way I came in, or I could continue to follow the two-track and hope it ended somewhere with a phone. It was a good five miles back to the laundromat, so I decided to walk where the road would take me. I took off my shoes, rolled up my pants, and sloshed my way through the mud.

There's nothing worse than feeling stuck and unable to move.

As I walked, I noticed that what I had thought was a cemetery was really more of a botanical garden. There were flowers and fruit trees, blueberry bushes, ornamental grasses, and neatly trimmed shrubbery all placed in little clusters within a well-manicured lawn. Rocks, bricks, and scalloped metal edging encircled the clusters, and the more I looked at the garden's beauty, the more a pattern began to emerge. Looking more closely, I could also see that vegetables of various kinds were scattered amidst the flowers and fruit trees, and the variegated heights and colors were very pleasing to the eye. If this was part of the Paradise Realty property, it lived up to its name!

About a half mile into my walk, I began to get little glimpses of the cottage peeking through the trees. It seemed bigger and newer than the place I was looking for, but I hoped that maybe they'd let me use their phone. As I got closer, I noticed that there was a gate in the fence reminiscent of the entrance to the cemetery that I saw last night.

A lot of people get bogged down with the busyness of life.

Two stone columns formed an arch over a heavy wooden gate. I tugged on the handle to the gate, but it was bolted and locked from the inside.

The road twisted its way down past the lake, so I walked out on someone's dock, dangled my feet in the water, and washed the mud off myself. The sun was breaking over the tree line, and it cast a long silver reflection on the rippled water. It was going to be a beautiful day.

I sat there for a few minutes enjoying the view. When I stood and turned around, I realized that someone had opened the gate, and there was a sign that said "Paradise Realty Open House," with Michael DeAngelo's picture on it.

Before I could say anything, Michael came walking through the gate and caught me by surprise. His presence seemed to fill my space, so I took a step back. He was tall and thick and athletically built, with longish black hair that flowed back from his widow's peak, like Tom Hanks in the movie *The Da Vinci Code.* There was a whisper of gray in his sideburns as well as his neatly trimmed mustache and goatee.

"I'm sorry," he said. "I didn't mean to startle you. There's no need to be frightened. I'm Michael, and we've been expecting you."

"Oh, yes, you're the agent. I recognize you from the picture."

A good salesman always makes you feel like he's on your side, and Michael was no exception. There was something charismatic about him. His words were soothing and persuasive, and you got the impression that he meant what he said.

Gathering my composure, I walked through the gate and up the sidewalk and knocked on the screen door.

"Well, come on in, Scout. We've been waiting for you," said a man from inside.

At first I wasn't sure he was talking to me. No one had called me that name in almost fifty years. Scout was the nickname my mother gave me as a toddler because I had a habit of breaking loose and running out ahead of everyone else unless she kept a firm grip on my little hand. It was not an admirable trait in her mind, and eventually she hooked a short piece of clothesline to my belt to rein me in whenever she took my sister and me shopping.

It must be a coincidence, I thought to myself. *He probably calls every guy "Scout" or "Sport" or something like that.*

The voice of the man who called me Scout sounded familiar. It was slow, deliberate, and deep, like Gregory Peck in *To Kill a Mockingbird*, but the man himself looked more like Paul Newman. He was tall, lean, and weathered, with steely blue eyes and short, cropped gray hair that receded slightly. He wore faded blue jeans, white Converse tennis shoes, and a green T-shirt that said "Save the Whales" on it. His shirt had the white dust of flour on it, and from the looks of him, I made him out to be the cook.

The screen door closed behind me, and I was standing in the kitchen. The room was filled with the alluring smell of freshly baked sticky buns. There was something familiar and yet foreign about this place. If it was the place of my memories, it had undergone an extensive remodel somewhere along the way. I'm not saying that it felt like home, but it was the kind of place you wanted to come home to. Then again, sometimes you can feel right at home in a place you've never been.

As I looked around, I saw flour, sugar, cinnamon, baking soda, and a bag of crushed walnuts scattered in disarray atop the counter, along with bowls of varying sizes sitting next to a mixer with beaters still covered with dough.

A block of butter, a pitcher of milk, brightly colored aluminum glasses, yellowed bone china plates, and an assortment of silverware were set on the table. The table itself was made of tubular chrome with a slate gray Formica top. One side was shoved tight against the wall, and three matching chairs were tucked neatly under the other three sides.

Sometimes you can feel right at home in a place you've never been.

The floor was wooden and worn. White beadboard went about five feet up the walls and was capped with a shelf that served as a plate rail. Above it, black-and-white photos leaned against a royal blue wall. The cupboards were white with glass doors that displayed an eclectic assortment of dishes and glasses. The appliances were white and rounded, bulbous, like the ones out of the fifties, although they appeared to be new.

"Come on in," the man said, motioning toward the table with his head. "I'll be frosting those sticky buns in a minute, and the milk is cold and fresh. I'm telling you, it's a little taste of heaven."

"You're in for a treat," said Michael, who had followed me in. "Ahbee bakes his cinnamon rolls from scratch, like everything else he makes."

"I'm sorry," I said. "I feel kind of foolish. I appreciate the invitation for breakfast, I really do, and I'd love to see the place—in fact, I came for the open house—but first I need a tow truck. You see, I got stuck in the mud last night, and I ended up sleeping in my car. So right now, all I really want to do is use your phone, okay?"

"Sure," answered Michael. "That's understandable. You don't need to explain it to us. We know what happened. People come knocking on our door all the time when they get stuck. We help them. We're always willing to help. But right now I'll bet your mind is buzzing with questions. Am I right?"

"Well, yes," I answered, somewhat puzzled. "That's exactly right. I'm a little confused. I know word gets around fast in a small town, but do I know you? Were you expecting me? What's this really about?"

"That's your department," Michael said to Ahbee. "You're in charge of ideas and answers. I'm just the messenger."

"Oh, there'll be lots of time for explanations later," the old one said, putting his hand on my shoulder. "I'm so glad you're here."

I wanted to ask where "here" was, but he never gave me a chance.

"Your room is ready," Ahbee continued. "Michael will show you where it is in a few minutes, but let's eat first. Sit down, sit down, you must be starving."

They each pulled out a chair while motioning for me to do the same, and for a moment we sat and smiled at each other in an awkward silence. Then Michael folded his hands, bowed his head, and said a word of grace. He thanked God for the day, for the food, and for my safe arrival, and when he said "Amen," the old man said, "You're welcome."

How odd, I thought to myself. I was beginning to feel a little uncomfortable. Something about all this was one bubble off plumb. But then it dawned on me: this was Carol's doing! She must have gone online and booked a room for me without telling me. That's so Carol. She loves to surprise me, and she knew more than anyone that what I needed was to get away for a few days. Sure, that must be it. That's why these two were expecting me. Little by little, the pieces were falling into place.

As I looked up, my eyes caught the old man's gaze, and for a moment it was as though he had peeked into my very soul. Clearly he knew much more than he was letting on. There was wisdom in his years, but I sensed that it was something that would have to be pried out of him a little bit at a time.

Without saying a word, Ahbee flipped the cinnamon rolls out of the pan, turned them nut-side down, and began frosting them with a cream cheese icing and serving them.

"I've heard of open houses where they baked a loaf of bread so the house would smell like home, but I've never heard of one where they served breakfast. It's a nice touch," I said, taking a bite of my cinnamon roll. "Homey—and it kind of makes me feel like I belong here."

"You do belong here," said Ahbee. "We have everything ready for your stay."

"Do I know you?" I asked again. "You look so familiar to me. Have we met before?"

"I imagine I do," Ahbee replied with a wry smile. "We've met many times." As he poured me a glass of milk, he said, "I knew your parents quite well. In fact, your father and I had quite a talk on the day you were born."

"You look to be about his age," I responded. "Were you and Dad friends when he was young? Have you known him a long time?"

"We're very close. Your grandmother introduced us when he was only a young boy."

"It's funny that he never mentioned you. Were you from the old neighborhood on College Avenue?" I asked.

"Oh, I know the old neighborhood very well," he replied. "And I'm sure you've heard your dad speak of me."

I began to get a little annoyed with what seemed to be an obvious evasion of my questions.

"Listen," I said. "I appreciate the hospitality, and the sticky bun was great. Actually, I've never had better. You were right, it tasted like a little bit of heaven. But this is the strangest open house I've ever been to. It's like I woke up in Neverland! Just where in the world am I, anyway?"

"Well, that's the point, isn't it?" the old man answered. "You've gotten away from it all here. Like the sign says, 'You're in God's country now.'"

"God's country?"

"You know, heaven," he said with a sincerity that was hard to deny. "And I'm opening my house to you. At least a part of it."

"And that makes you—"

"I Am," he interrupted.

I couldn't help but hear an echo of Exodus where Moses asks God his name and the Lord replies, "I AM WHO I AM." My preacher likes to throw a little Hebrew into his sermons, and I remember him saying that God's answer was the Hebrew verb "to be" twice repeated. According to him it can be translated "I am," or "I was," or "I will be," or any combination of the three. In some ways, it was both an answer and a refusal to answer. It's both open-ended and open to interpretation.

When God told Moses that he was the great I Am, in some ways, it was both an answer and a refusal to answer.

It was like God was messing with Moses by speaking in riddles, and I was beginning to feel the way Moses must have felt.

"Look," I said, "I don't know if this is some kind of game, or who you people are, but maybe I should go check on my car."

With that, I got up and walked out the door.

choices

Your life is the sum result of all the choices you make, both consciously and unconsciously. If you can control the process of choosing, you can take control of all aspects of your life.

Robert F. Bennett

2

It was a beautiful day. The sun was shining, the birds were singing, and a gentle breeze blew the screen door shut as I walked down the brick path and out the gate. The two-track followed the line of the lakeshore for about a quarter of a mile and then merged into Old Mill Road. On the left side of the road there was a public swimming beach with a sign that said SWIM AT YOUR OWN RISK, and to the right was the beach parking lot. I didn't know where I was, but it all felt strangely familiar, like I'd been there before.

As I got closer, I could see my car sitting in the far corner of the lot with the door open. Someone had pulled it out of the mud, washed it off, and parked it next to the row of rusted rural route mailboxes. The top was down, the keys were in the ignition, and there was a piece of paper under the windshield wiper that I assumed was the tow bill. Instead, it was a note that said, "Look inside the mailbox."

When I glanced back at the row of old mailboxes, one of them had my name on it. Hand-painted in weathered black block letters it said DR. SCHUYLER HUNT. Tentatively, I looked inside. There I found a brown manila envelope with Ed McMahon's picture on it. It too had my name on it, and stamped in red it said, "You may already be a winner!"

There's something reassuring about getting mail, even if it's only the electric bill. It says someone's thinking about you, someone cares about you, you matter, and we all hunger for that. Insecurity is the common thread that links humanity. I had left the cottage because I'd felt uncomfortable, but getting the letter had the opposite effect.

Carol had sent me on a few wild goose chases in my life, but this was a little out there even for her. Still, somehow she must have known that I'd be a little uncomfortable with Michael and the old man, so she sent the letter to soothe my worries. I held it for a moment and then broke open the seal. Inside was a picture of the cottage that I'd just left, and below it was written, "The path goes in two directions. One is safe and well-traveled; the other holds the answers that you seek most. Either way, the choice is yours."

> *Insecurity is the common thread that links humanity.*

For what seemed like an eternity, I stood by the mailbox. Looking down, I realized that there were indeed many footprints heading off in front of me. As I turned around, only my footprints were left in the sand behind me. A voice in my head said, *Don't be a fool—take the safe path. Those others couldn't all have been wrong.* It didn't make sense. Why should I be the one to break from the pack?

But then again, I've never been one to play it safe. I've spent my life ignoring the warnings, speeding up on yellow, and rushing headlong into a challenge. In fact, that's always been a problem for me. I have a hard time letting things go. When I was a kid, my dad always told me to go for it, to throw caution to the wind, to run at a problem instead of running away from it, and it's become second nature to me. I guess I could say that it's probably my father's fault.

On my first day of school in seventh grade, I left the house with fifty cents in my pocket, hoping to buy the school lunch. Why I wanted to do that is a wonderment to me now, but at the time, not carrying a brown bag lunch seemed like a big deal.

When the lunch bell rang at eleven fifty, Rodney Williams asked me if I had lunch money. When I told him I did, he demanded that I give it to him.

Some people play it safe, and some people speed up on yellow.

Did I mention that this was Rodney's second trip to seventh grade and that he'd spent two years in third grade as well? That meant the two of us were on the opposite ends of puberty. He was big, strong, and hairy, and I—well, let's just say that I wasn't.

Not being all that streetwise, I tried to explain to Rodney that if I gave him my lunch money I wouldn't get a sandwich. "If you don't give it to me, I'll give you a *knuckle* sandwich," he replied, holding up a fist the size of a softball.

Needless to say, I didn't eat lunch that day.

That night I told my dad what had happened and explained to him that I needed a dollar for lunch—fifty cents for my new best friend, Rodney, and fifty cents for me. Although he sympathized with my dilemma, Dad said that I would only be getting fifty cents for lunch and that I had two choices: I could hit Rodney as hard as I could in the nose, or I could go hungry.

"If I hit him," I said, "he'll kill me."

"If you don't, he'll eat your lunch every day," Dad replied.

I lay awake that night worrying and wondering what to do. I even prayed that Rodney would be sick or not very hungry. Evidently God wasn't listening, because when the lunch bell rang at eleven fifty, Rodney made a beeline for my desk.

He said what I knew he'd say. "Have you got your—"

Bang! I hit ol' Rodney as hard as I could, and he went down like an elevator. He banged his head on the radiator, and when his head hit the tile floor, it sounded like someone dropped a bowling ball.

What did I do? What could I do? I jumped on top of him and pummeled him in the face until the science teacher, Mr. Pulte, pulled me off and dragged me down to the principal's office.

The principal's name was Elmo Wiersma, and he looked like an Elmo. He had receding black curly hair, high cheekbones, and a long, pointy nose with bifocals balanced on the end. I soon learned that Elmo had zero tolerance for fighting.

"What possessed you to hit poor Rodney?" he asked.

"My dad told me to," I explained.

"Listen, young man, I'm in no mood for games! If I don't start getting a straight answer, I'm going to suspend you for three days and call your dad."

"Go ahead and call him," I replied.

And he did.

The conversation started off pleasant enough. "I'm sorry to bother you, Mr. Hunt, but your boy is in my office for fighting, and he says you told him to."

For a moment there was an awkward silence, followed by a "Hmm" and an "I see," after which Mr. Wiersma got a pained look on his face. "But that's no reason to return violence for violence," he said. "I'm afraid I'll have to suspend him for three days. I have no other choice."

I don't know what my dad said next, but ol' Elmo's face got as red as a tomato, and I heard him say, "Well, Mr. Hunt, if that's the way you feel, then he's suspended for the whole week." And he hung up.

When my dad picked me up from school, we went out for ice cream, and he said, "We don't need to share this with your mother, right, Scout?"

"Right!" I answered.

When I went back to school the next week, Rodney confronted me just like my dad said he would.

"You better watch your back!"

Inside I was terrified, but I said what Dad told me to say: "You want a little more of what you got before?"

Rodney looked at me for a minute, turned, and walked away saying again that I'd better watch my back, but I could tell that he was more afraid of me now than I was of him. It seemed I'd developed a reputation. From then on, everyone said I was either crazy or tough. No one was quite sure which, but either way, they didn't want to mess with me anymore, and I ate hot lunch all year.

After that, I didn't have much use for playing it safe, and whenever there was a problem, I ran at it, not away from it. So like I said, it's probably Dad's fault.

The Bible says that before they were kicked out of paradise, Adam and Eve talked with God in the Garden. There within the gates of Eden, each afternoon, in the cool of the day, they asked their questions, and God answered. We don't know what their questions were, but we know what ours are, and my guess is that many of them would be the same. *Why* questions, and *when* questions, and even *how* questions.

We all have questions we'd like God to answer, and maybe that's what eternity is all about.

I've always had lots of questions, and I don't think I'm alone. I think there's a part of each of us that was born homesick for Eden. Like Adam and Eve, we want to walk peacefully among the lilies, the leopard, the lion, and the lamb and get our questions answered. I can't imagine how long it would take to answer all our questions, but maybe that's what eternity is all about.

Back at the mailbox, curiosity won out over fear, and I found myself slowly retracing my footsteps back toward the cottage.

As I got closer, I noticed what I'd missed before. The sign above the entrance said Angel's Gate.

Yes, I thought to myself. *That confirms it. This is the place I read about on the internet.*

I wished that Carol could see it. The house itself was old but well-maintained. From the outside, it looked more like a home than an inn. It was a large saltbox with a carriage house attached to the back. The grounds were well-kept, surrounded by flowers and fruit trees and a large, towering pine.

The building sat atop a slight knoll, with stone steps cut in the hill on the front side. A brick walkway went out through the gate and led down to the lake. I was admiring its beauty and haunted by a lost memory that perhaps I'd been there before, when suddenly I realized that Michael was standing beside me.

"You have a way of sneaking up on people," I said. "Where'd you come from, anyway?"

He ignored my question and opened the gate, and together we walked up the path. As we went through the kitchen door, he said, "Like Ahbee, I'm always around, even if you're not looking for me."

Ahbee interrupted just as I was going to ask Michael what he meant by that.

"I'm so glad you decided to come back."

"Did I have a choice?" I asked.

"Of course. You always have a choice. I simply tried to help you make the right choice," Ahbee answered.

"I'll bet you're the one who put my name on that mailbox, aren't you?" I questioned.

"Yes," he answered. "I knew your name before you did, and I also knew you couldn't resist looking inside. You've always been more curious than cautious."

"And the letter?" I asked. "Did you and Carol come up with that?"

"No, she had nothing to do with it. This is strictly between you and me."

"Look," I said, frustrated. "I don't know what's going on here, but it seems to me that you both know a lot more about me than

I do about you. So why don't you guys quit fooling around and fill in some of the blanks for me?"

"Oh, you know us much better than you think!" Ahbee said. "That's part of your problem. You're overthinking this. It is what it is. Nothing more, nothing less."

"If that's true," I replied, "then either you've gone to a lot of trouble to get me here, or this is all some kind of a weird dream."

"Would you be more comfortable if it was a dream?" the old one asked.

"No. I just want to know if this is real or not."

"Oh, it's real all right," he replied. "As real as a root canal, probably the most real thing you've ever done. And parts of it will be painful, but in the end you'll be better for it."

"That's right," Michael chimed in. "No harm will come to you here, I can promise you that, and you're free to leave anytime you want."

"Well, if this is so real and so wonderful, then where in the world am I?"

"Like I tried to tell you before," Ahbee continued, "think of this as a little taste of heaven on earth. Time has no meaning here. This will be like a seamless gap in your story."

"My story?"

"Every life is a story," Ahbee explained. "Some people think their story is predetermined. They imagine that every line of the script of their lives was written by someone else. They have no choice, no responsibility. They're simply actors in the play, part of a predestined plot. Others see themselves as the author. They imagine that they are in charge of their own life, the master of their fate and the captain of their soul."

"So which is it?" I asked. "You seem to have this figured out, so tell me—is life a matter of choice, or is it predestined?"

"It's a mixture of both. The problem is in knowing where the one drops off and the other begins. Each life is a story in time, but not all stories are the same. For example, some people, older people, often want to stop time. They live in the past, and their story always begins with the words, 'Once upon a time, a long, long time ago.'

"For others, for the very young, it's the opposite. They want to speed up time. They're in a hurry to get on with it. For them the story is always about tomorrow, and it always begins, 'Someday.' Sometimes they're so concerned about tomorrow that they can't enjoy today."

Ahbee continued. "Everybody's story is a drama unfolding in the moment. Often, when they get written down, the stories begin with the words, 'It was a dark and stormy night,' for the times most people remember are the times of mystery, tragedy, danger, and uncertainty. But everyone's story has both ups and downs, triumphs and tears, moments of clarity and times of uncertainty. Time is both your friend and your enemy."

Slowly I slumped into one of the kitchen chairs, trying to make some sense of what they were saying, and that's when I realized that the clock on the stove had no hands.

"Time may not mean anything here," Michael said, "but it means everything in your world. It's an unrenewable resource, and it should never be wasted. Even now, time is winding down there. We've always been very clear about that. The prophets of the Hebrew testament and the writers of the new one have all said that the world was designed with a beginning, a middle, and an end. And Ahbee has always said that when it's over, he will bring you to himself. Meanwhile, it's my job to go back and forth as his messenger and to be the keeper of the gate."

Time is an unrenewable resource that should never be wasted.

That's when it hit me. Everything fell into place. *DeAngelo*—this guy thinks he's the archangel, Michael!

"I didn't know angels sold real estate," I said.

"You made that assumption on your own," Michael replied.

"All I said was that I was Ahbee's agent. Over the years, I have been called many things: his messenger, his agent, his angel, his gatekeeper. It's all the same to me."

"What do you mean, 'gatekeeper'?" I asked.

"Since Adam broke the relationship with Ahbee, I've been under strict orders. No one enters paradise except by invitation. Of course, most come through the front gate; their invitation is for eternity, and it's written in the blood of the Lamb. But some, like you, are invited by Ahbee on a temporary visa. You come through my gate, the angel's gate, the back door of heaven."

"I didn't know heaven had a back door."

"There are a lot of things you don't know," Michael said. "But hopefully, some of that will change over the next few days."

I must admit that I didn't really believe a word of it, but I was intrigued by it all.

Michael was wearing faded blue jeans, a crisp white shirt, a black corduroy jacket, and a pair of brown penny loafers.

"You don't look like any angel I've ever seen," I said.

"Really?" Michael asked. "And just how many angels have you seen? Remember the night when you crawled into that sewer pipe that ran under the road over by Redeemer College? You were eleven at the time, and you couldn't resist chasing after that green speckled frog. You kept stretching out your arm, reaching your way into the pipe until you were good and stuck. You couldn't go forward or backward, remember? Little by little, fear had its way with you, and you began to panic."

For a moment Michael leaned back in his chair with a smirk on his face, and then he went on with his story. "You shouted, 'Help me, God! Send your angels to save me!' And that's exactly what he did. Of course, one angel was more than sufficient, and the task was given to me. Even now, you distinctly remember someone tugging on your leg, but when you turned around, I was gone. We angels are a little bashful," he explained. "We don't show ourselves unless Ahbee tells us to.

"No," Michael continued, "as far as I know, you've never actually seen an angel. Even the afternoon of the accident."

"How did you know about that sewer pipe?" I asked. "I've never told anyone about that. And if you're suggesting that God was there at the lake the day of Ben's accident, then why didn't he do something? If there was ever a God-forsaken day, that was it."

"Never in your life have you been God-forsaken, not even for a minute. Even in the midst of tragedy, Ahbee is with you. He doesn't always keep you from falling, but he's always there to help you up when you do. As for the details of your life, they are meticulously monitored and recorded, and they can be recounted at any time."

"You are amazed that we know about the night a frightened boy cried out in fear, or the afternoon his brother cried out in pain," said the old one. "But I tell you, you will see things that are much more amazing than that if you decide to stay."

Much of the pain and suffering of our world is the result of poor choices.

"Do I have a choice?" I asked once again.

"You always have a choice," Michael replied. "Ahbee wouldn't have it any other way. Much of the pain and suffering in your world is the result of poor choices, but he never forces anyone to do the right thing.

"He leads, he warns, he influences," Michael continued, "but he never makes anyone do anything. The conspiracy is not our doing, I can assure you of that."

"What conspiracy?"

"We'll talk more about that later, but first things first. For now, let me show you around."

"Later?" I asked. "I thought time had no meaning here. Besides, Carol will be home in a few days, and she'll be worried if I'm not there."

"Don't worry," he said assuredly. "You'll be home long before she is. Besides, like I said, time doesn't matter here, but for your sake, we'll divide your stay up into day and night. And yes, it's fun for us too. It reminds us of how those began, but that's also a story for another time. For now, let's take a walk."

Michael led me through the room where he had entered before. What I thought was a parlor was in fact part of a U-shaped living room that wrapped around three sides of a huge Rumford stone fireplace. The stairway mirrored the shape of the room, circling around the back of the fireplace, and

God never forces us to do the right thing.

ended at the second floor. The west end of the room was a library of sorts. It contained a table, a lamp, and an old, comfortable-looking leather chair, all of which sat on a beautiful Persian rug. The archway and the west wall were lined with bookshelves, floor to ceiling.

I recognized many of the volumes and slowed to read the titles of others. A ladder on wheels followed a track that was hooked around what had to be at least a ten-foot ceiling. I spotted a volume that looked for the life of me like the bound copy of a book I had started writing in college. At the time I had visions of writing the great American novel, but I never got around to finishing it. I started to climb the ladder for a close look, but Michael said, "I know the power books have over you, but now's not the time for reading."

Mission-style furniture filled the larger southern wing of the living room. A chocolate-colored leather couch with plaid pillows, two end tables, a grandfather clock, and a red recliner lined the opposite wall, which was really a series of sliding glass doors that opened to a screened-in porch overlooking the lake.

"This is my favorite room in the whole house," Michael said as we stepped across the threshold.

The screens were neatly tucked inside the stone columns that narrowed as they rose, and white wicker furniture filled the space.

White and watermelon-colored pillows sat in the seat of a rocker, a porch swing, and two high chairs around a glass-topped table. The big pine cast its shadow across the entire front of the house, shielding it from the sun, and a gentle breeze rustled the leaves on the fruit trees outside and freshened the air on the porch. It was beautiful looking out over the lake, and I couldn't help but wonder if it was always so pleasant there.

"I love it out here," Michael said, as if he read my mind. "There's always a breeze blowing."

Pointing out to a small aluminum rowboat tied to the dock out front, he said, "Feel free to go fishing if you want. The boat is at your disposal. There are poles and tackle in the carriage house out back. But if I know you, you're probably more interested in exploring that library, right?"

"Right," I answered, turning to glance back at the books. But when I turned around again, Michael was gone.

I walked back inside to the library, grabbed a book on ancient Egyptian archaeology, sat down in the leather chair, and began reading.

perseverance

If I had to select one quality, one personal characteristic that I regard as being most highly correlated with success, whatever the field, I would pick the trait of perseverance.

Rich DeVos

3

The next thing I knew, Michael was gently shaking my shoulder and asking if I was hungry.

"Sure am," I said. "What's for supper?"

"You'll have to ask the cook," he said. "He's out front by the grill."

As I got up to go outside, I caught a glimpse out the west window of a butter yellow '67 Chevy Camaro RS Convertible. I've always been a car buff, even when I was a little kid, and I couldn't resist taking the long way around to the front yard so I could take a closer look at the Camaro.

I could smell the smoke of the charcoal grill as I went out the screen door in the kitchen, and I could feel my stomach growl. I hadn't had lunch and I was really starting to get hungry. But the sight of that Camaro made me forget about my appetite. She was a beauty, and in mint shape too.

The first thing I noticed was the raised red-letter tires. "I haven't seen those in a long time," I said to myself. "This must belong to a serious collector." The car had polished chrome lake pipes running along the rockers and chrome reverse rims. The inside was leather, and there was a Beach Boys eight-track tape lying on the passenger's seat.

A familiar voice called out to me, "We can take her for a ride after dinner if you want."

As I turned around, I thought my eyes were playing tricks on me. It sounded like Roz, and it looked like him too, or to be more accurate, he looked like he'd looked in his younger years. This man was in his thirties, so it couldn't be Roz, because he had been in his seventies when he died ten years ago. His wife Myra (Mike to her friends) had worked with my mom at Interstate when they were both in their twenties, and when they got together socially, my dad and Roz hit it off immediately. Both of them loved to hunt and fish, and they were both in the auto industry.

Roz started a company called Autocast about the same time Dad started Capitol Engineering. Money was tight in my childhood years, but we weren't aware of it. Our families would get together every other Saturday night and we'd have a wienie roast or an Indian corn boil, or sometimes we'd just play board games, make popcorn, and watch *Gunsmoke* on TV. Those were good memories, but that was almost fifty years ago, and the man in front of me was twenty years younger than I was.

The sun was to his back, and I could make out the silhouette of a big man with curly hair. He wore Red Wing boots, khaki pants, and a short-sleeved, powder-blue silk shirt with wide lapels and an open collar.

Whoever he was, he was big and strong, with arms like tree trunks. In his prime, Roz was two hundred fifty pounds, and it was all muscle. He used to say that he was "an eighth of a ton of trouble and fun," which was really true! Like Roz, the man by the grill had a neatly trimmed, pencil-thin mustache riding above his grin.

"It's all right, boy," he said. "Come on over here, and let me have a look at you."

Then he laughed. That's when I knew it really was him. Roz

had a great laugh. At first I didn't know whether to laugh or cry, but when he caught me up in a bear hug, I cried like a baby. I'd forgotten how much I missed him. He was always one of those people you could lean into when times got tough.

"How can this be?" I asked. "You're dead and gone!"

"Well, I'm gone, that's for sure. Then again, as you can see, I'm here, aren't I? I know it seems kind of confusing, but I'll explain what I can and leave the rest for the others."

"Others?" I asked.

"Sure," he answered. "You didn't think I was the only one with an invitation to come and eat with you, did you?"

"Frankly, I don't know what to think."

"That's going to take some time," Roz replied. "For now, I think the steaks are just about ready."

The line between life and death is not as crisp and clean as we might imagine.

We walked over to the grill where there were two porterhouse steaks the size of dinner plates and four ears of corn still in the husks.

"A little pink in the middle all right?" he asked.

"Perfect," I answered.

Roz put a steak on my plate along with an ear of corn, and we walked over and sat down on the front steps.

"Still use ketchup?"

"Still do."

"It's over there on that little folding table," Roz said.

On the table were salt and pepper, Heinz ketchup, and a Mason jar three quarters full of water with an inch of melted butter floating on top.

I peeled back the husk on my corn, revealing the familiar purple, blue, and yellow kernels.

"Field corn?" I asked. "I haven't had this in years!"

"Yeah, well, you know how it is," Roz said. "Old habits are hard to break. Besides, it sounds more exotic if you call it Indian corn."

When I was a kid, we'd sometimes go over to their house in the country and that's all we'd have for supper. We'd dip the ears in the Mason jar and they'd come out slathered in butter. By the time we were done, our faces would be covered in salt and pepper, and butter would be rolling down our chins. Afterward, there would be homemade ice cream for dessert.

"After supper what do you say we go for a ride?" Roz asked. "You crank, and I'll drive."

"Crank?"

"You've got to do something to earn your dessert," he said. "Besides, that ice cream isn't going to make itself."

The two of us caught up over dinner, and afterward I learned exactly how hard I was going to have to work to earn my dessert. Roz put milk, eggs, crushed ice, and other ingredients in a wooden bucket. Then he snapped the lid on top and said, "Here you go." There was a quart of fresh strawberries on the floor in front of my seat. They were mashed up and mixed with brown sugar, and I assumed that when the ice cream got a little harder we'd pour them on top, just like we did when I was a kid.

We drove east in front of the cottage as the sun set behind us. The side pipes on the Camaro rumbled as the Beach Boys' favorite hits played on the eight-track. Neither of us said a word until we rolled to a stop at the end of the road. Roz told me that the place was called Promise Point.

"This is a great place to go fishing," he said, and as I looked around there was something strangely familiar about it. It was a grass-covered finger of land that jutted out about a tenth of a mile into the lake. Cattails hugged the edge of the shore, and two large white pines stood like soldiers on sentry duty on the beach at the end of the point. The two of us made our way out to a weathered old picnic table that sat beneath the pines.

When we sat down I noticed that someone had carved their initials in it years ago along with the words "I PROMISE" in capital letters. I wondered if the promise was ever kept, but before

I could say anything, Roz started dishing up the ice cream and berries and said, "Okay, Scout, I know you've got questions, so ask away."

"I'm not sure where to start," I said. "But okay. Why am I here? How are you here? And where the heck is 'here' anyway?"

"All I really know," he replied, "is that each of us has something for you, something you can take back and share if you want to. What I've got, you already know. I'm supposed to remind you that *God's not done with you yet*. He has so much more in store for you."

"That's it? That's all? God's not done with me yet?"

God's not done with you yet. He has so much more in store for you.

"Let me see if I can help you understand this a little better," Roz replied. "Remember when you were little and I took you to my dad's shop?"

"Sure. That's the first time I ever sat on a horse."

Roz was really named Roswell Boyce Stillwater III. His dad, R. B., was a blacksmith, as were his grandfather and his great-grandfather.

"Well, life is like that," Roz continued. "Dad would grab hold of those shoes, stick them in the fire, and mold and shape them until they conformed to the shape he wanted. Some of them were made for plow horses, some for racehorses, some for show, and some for ice and snow. Each shoe took the shape it needed to best do its job.

"Now, if you were to ask one of those shoes if they liked going through the fire or being hammered into shape, my guess is they'd say no, but it was necessary. And sometimes it's the same way with us. We've got to go through some of that if we're going to conform to the life God wants us to live. Does that make sense?"

"Some," I said. "But why does it have to be so hard?"

"That all goes back to a garden and a decision that you might not ever totally understand, at least not for a while."

51

Roz went on. "Remember how I showed you those old horseshoes that my grandfather put in the crotch of that tree?"

"Oh, yeah, I remember. The tree grew right around them."

"And that's my point. When we stop doing what God made us to do, we sort of get swallowed up by the busyness of life, and then whatever goals, dreams, and aspirations we might have had can evaporate. Our souls get trampled on by the lesser things of life.

"In many ways," Roz continued, "life is like a marathon race. There's a starting line and a finish line, but the race is won or lost somewhere in between the two. Everyone is enthusiastic and hopeful at the starting line, and as they cross the finish line, whether they win a medal or not, there is a feeling of accomplishment. But races are won and lost in between, in the middle miles. When your legs ache, and your chest heaves, and you're not sure you have what it takes to finish. That's when you discover what you're really made of. And that's the way it works in life too."

When we stop doing what God created us to do, the goals, dreams, and aspirations he has for us get swallowed up by life.

As he spoke I nodded in agreement. There was a part of me that had been stuck in the middle ever since Ben's accident. I knew that I had to figure out a way to get past it, but the problem was, I didn't really know where to start. Here I was a psychologist with a successful Christian counseling practice. I was the guy people came to when they couldn't get past this kind of stuff, and ironically, I couldn't get past it myself. That thought caused me to listen with even greater intensity as Roz continued talking.

"When I first started out in business," he said, "it was hard. I put in long hours for little money, but Myra and I were excited about the possibilities. We were chasing the American dream. I went to work every day fueled by the adrenaline of being my own boss, of being in business for myself. And years later, when we'd made it, there was this great feeling of accomplishment. We felt blessed. We felt like God had been with us every step of the way. We felt good knowing that we'd done what we set out to do and that it was better than we'd ever dreamed it would be.

"But during the in-between years, when I was working late every night, when the kids were growing up and I wasn't around to see it, it didn't always seem so great. We were living in an old farmhouse, bills were piling up, and there were lots of nights when I wondered if we'd make it, if it was worth it, and if I should give up and go to work for someone else.

"Now, looking back, it all seems so crystal clear, but at the time it wasn't. There were days when we were just feeling our way along, taking life one day at a time. And what I'm saying is, that's the way life works. We do most of our living in between. In between relationships, in between jobs, in between where we were and where we're going. And along the way you may have days when you feel like quitting, days when you wonder why God doesn't step in and give you some kind of sign. It's on those days I want you to remember that *God's not done with you yet*. I know it's been rough lately, and in the race of life the in-between miles always seem the longest and the steepest, but hang in there, don't give up, because he has some amazing things in store for you."

In the race of life, the middle miles always seem longest.

With that, he pointed to the Camaro and said, "I've got to get you back."

As he turned the car around, I reached over and shut off the eight-track and said, "Roz, thanks for coming. You don't know how much it means to me. But I've got one more question."

"Shoot!" he said.

"Is God Paul Newman?"

"No, but he sure looks like him, doesn't he?"

"Yeah," I said. "And he sounds like Gregory Peck."

"I've noticed that too, but when I've come for supper when other people were staying here, he hasn't always looked like that. In fact, the last time I was here, he looked like Charlton Heston and he sounded like Morgan Freeman. I think he slips on the costume that best fits our expectations. I once heard Paul say that he was all things to all people so he might save some, and I imagine that it's the same way with God. He reveals himself to us in many different ways, but we don't always recognize him.

God reveals himself to us in many different ways, but we don't always recognize him.

As Jesus once said, 'Let those with ears hear, and those with eyes see.' Does that help you, Scout?"

"Lately, I've seen more than I've understood," I replied.

"Sometimes that's the way it works," Roz responded. "But wisdom comes to those who wait."

After that we didn't say much, and on the way back we listened to the eight-track and replayed old memories in our minds. It was well after dark by the time we got back to the cottage.

"It was good to see you, Scout," Roz said as we stood on the little porch outside the kitchen.

"Aren't you coming inside?" I asked.

"No, I've got to get going, but I'm really glad we had this time." Then he put his arm around me, gave me a hug, and said, "Go on in, they're waiting for you."

With that, he walked back to the Camaro and got in.

"Tell Myra I'll be waiting for her," he yelled as he rambled down the drive. "And tell the kids what I told you. Oh, and one other thing . . . Cut Ben a little slack, will you? God's not finished with him yet either. Ben's just not quite as far along in his race as you are. He's had a few tough breaks—some were his fault, and some weren't. He's starting to get his game together. Give him a little time. You'll see, you'll see."

I watched until the bullet-shaped taillights faded out of sight, and then I turned and walked inside.

questions

It is not every question that deserves an answer.

Publilius Syrus

4

As I walked in the screen door to the kitchen, Michael was sitting at the table.

"You must be tired," he said. "I'll show you where your room is."

We walked through the library past a smoldering fire and up the staircase to the second floor. The landing was a six-by-six-foot area. Three doors led to bedrooms and one went to a bathroom. Each door had a window above it that tilted in to allow the air to circulate. Like in the kitchen, the doors and wood trim were white. Again beadboard lined the walls, but here the wall above it was painted a dark khaki color.

Michael motioned toward the west bedroom and said, "This room is yours. You'll find clothes in the dresser, and the towels and toiletries in the bathroom are for you as well."

As I opened the door to my room, a slight breeze blew in. I turned to say thank you, but Michael was already gone.

Inside there was an oak dresser, a blue tweed wingback chair, and two twin beds covered in blue-and-white checked quilts. It looked kind of like the room Ben and I shared as kids at the cottage. The book I'd started reading that morning sat open on the dresser to the page I'd read last, and next to it was an old picture of Carol and me and the girls. Kate and Kelly wore matching green corduroy dresses that Carol had made, and Tara was a toddler.

I was in grad school then, but even though we really had to pinch our pennies, I remember those years as some of the best of our lives. Jesus once told the rich young ruler to sell everything he had and then come follow him. We had done just that—or at least we had chased the dream we thought God had planted in our hearts—and there was something exuberant about it. We knew deep down in our bones that the reward would one day outweigh the cost. I still believe that, but I'm not sure I'd be ready to do it again at this stage of my life. You get cautious when you get older. Maybe it's because you know what it costs to try to start over again in life, or maybe it's because you've got more to lose.

When Jesus left this life to go to the next, he promised to prepare a place for us also.

If this was heaven, then the good news was that they were expecting me. I couldn't help but be reminded that when Jesus left this life to go to the next, he promised to prepare a place for us also. After changing clothes, I lay on the bed, looked up at the stars, and started to say my prayers. "My Father which art in heaven—am I in heaven too?" I fell asleep before I finished the prayer.

In the morning, I awoke to the smell of coffee and bacon. The sun was shining, and I felt great. I can't remember the last time I slept that well. I got up, grabbed the robe, and walked across the hall to the bathroom. I splashed some water in my face and squeezed some toothpaste onto the brush, rolling it from the bottom like I always do. I started brushing my teeth and then glanced up at the mirror.

To my surprise, the man looking back at me was much younger than I am. It was me, but it wasn't, or at least it wasn't who I'd been for a long time. My hair was longer, thicker, and blonder.

The crow's-feet had disappeared from around my eyes, my cheeks were tan, and my chin was more pronounced. I looked like I did twenty-five years ago. I couldn't help but laugh out loud.

I remembered reading somewhere that Thomas Aquinas believed we'd all be thirty-three years old in heaven because that's how old Jesus was at the resurrection—old enough to avoid the foolish mistakes of youth, and young enough to avoid the pain and suffering of old age. It looked like the old saint was right!

I walked back to my room whistling and started to get dressed. I grabbed a Noah's Ark T-shirt and a pair of shorts, but then I noticed the size. They were 34s, and I was a snug 36. "Well, they don't get everything right here," I said to myself. But when I tried them on, they fit with room to spare. My hair might have been thicker, but my waist was definitely thinner.

I bounced down the stairs and walked into the dining room where the table was already set for breakfast. There was a large, round, light maple table with six ladder-back chairs. Six more chairs hung from hooks on the wall, suggesting that the table could be expanded as needed. Next to the table was a matching sideboard with leaded glass doors, and a large vase of fresh cut flowers sat on top of it. A watercolor painting of three children playing at the beach was hanging on the wall. "That looks like my sister, my brother, and me," I said.

Thomas Aquinas believed we'd all be thirty-three in heaven.

"It is!" said a voice from the kitchen. I was expecting to see Ahbee making breakfast, but instead, a Middle Eastern man in his thirties walked out smiling. He was wearing cuffed blue jeans, Keen sandals, and a well-worn gray T-shirt that said "Lowe's" on the pocket.

"I'm Josh," he said with a bit of an accent, and he extended his hand, swallowing mine in a crushing grip. I couldn't help but notice that his calloused hands were scarred and twisted, like he'd been in some kind of industrial accident.

"Sky," he said, "it is so good to have you here."

Once again, I felt at a disadvantage. Whoever this was, he seemed to know me.

"I am Ahbee's son," he said, as if he were reading my thoughts. "And he has asked me to spend some time with you today."

As I looked more carefully at the young man before me, I saw a definite family resemblance. He looked like a younger version of Ahbee, but taller. His skin was more olive in tone, his nose more pronounced, and his eyes were the color of baking chocolate. His words and his appearance were inviting. There was something magnetic about the man, and it made you want to get to know him better.

"Where are my manners?" he continued. "Sit down, sit down! How do you want your eggs?"

"I'm not sure," I said. "I usually have fruit for breakfast, and maybe some whole grain cereal. I've got to watch my cholesterol, you know."

"Not here, you don't! How about we make them sunny-side up along with an order of heavenly hash browns?"

"Sounds good to me!"

When he handed me the plate, it also had orange slices and four strips of bacon, crispy and crumbling, just the way I like it. The hash browns were shaped into a patty, and when I cut into them, there was in fact hash inside, along with a finely minced onion and a little yellow pepper. I bowed my head and prayed, "Thank you, Lord, for this day and for this food."

Like Ahbee, the young man said, "You're welcome."

"Aren't you going to eat?" I asked.

"I already ate," Josh replied. "But I'll break bread with you." As he reached across the table and grabbed a loaf of freshly baked whole grain bread, again I noticed the scars on his hands.

I was still uncertain where I was and who I was with, but clearly this was a place of wonderment.

"Should I call you Jesus?" I asked, testing my suspicions.

"You may," he answered. "But Joshua is the name my mother gave me, and so nowadays most everyone just calls me Josh."

"That would be Mary?" I asked.

"Of course," he responded. "Of course, you know her name as well as I."

"And the Keens?" I continued. "Aren't they a little out of costume for you?"

"I've always been a sandal man," Josh answered. "And the Keens are very comfortable."

I remained skeptical, but if this Josh was who he said he was, I had lots of questions for him.

"What do you want to do today?" Josh asked.

"I didn't know it was up to me," I retorted. "I thought you guys set the agenda here."

"No, it's like Michael said, 'The choice is yours'—it's always yours."

"Well then, if it's up to me, I'd like to spend a little time with you."

"Sounds good," Josh replied. "Sounds very good."

I had hoped we'd spend our time talking about the suffering of the world and the second coming. Sin and suffering were two things that I'd seen more than my share of in the last twenty-five years. When I started out as a staff psychologist at the state prison in Easton, I saw it played out in every session. Every inmate there had been both a victim and a predator at some point in their lives, and their stories haunted my dreams and almost strangled my faith in humanity. It got especially bad for me when I started seeing people I'd recommended for release come back as repeat offenders in only a matter of months.

We talked a lot of Jesus there, especially in the lifer's wing, but it had little effect on how most of them lived their lives. Clearly evil was more present in that place than anywhere I'd ever been, and eventually I knew I had to get out of there.

I thought it would be better when I started working in the

psych ward at Silver Ridge Hospital, but it wasn't. Evil simply popped up in other ways. This time it was more the evil of the system than the people. Over and over again I found myself asking God to do something, or at least to give us enough time to do something that made a difference in these people's lives, but sadly most of my prayers seemed to go unanswered. The insurance ran out before we could make any real progress, and most people went home with their demons in tow.

Eventually cynicism won out and I went into private practice, mostly for the money. Still, partly to appease my guilty conscience, and partly because it was who I wanted to be, I called it the Christian Compass Counseling Center and added the byline "Helping people find their way back on the right path." That's truly what I wanted to do, even what I felt called to do, and for a while at least I felt like that was what I was doing, but somewhere along the way I started to realize that the only permanent solution to the suffering of the world was the second coming of Jesus.

And then, by some mysterious twist of fate, I found myself walking beside the very one who could do something about it all. Unfortunately, instead of doing it, Josh wanted to walk up the hill behind the cottage in silence. I had so many questions and so many suggestions for what he might do, but I knew if that kind of a conversation was going to take place, he would have to start it.

To my great disappointment, he didn't. The two of us spent the day silently cutting lumber at the old sawmill that overlooked the garden. After a couple hours of sawdust and silence I began to feel a sense of accomplishment in this simple task that I hadn't felt in a long time. I marveled as I watched how efficiently Josh worked the wood through the saw. His movements were fluid and purposeful, with no wasted energy whatsoever. There was a gracefulness to his steps, almost like a ballet, and even though the work was exhausting, it was also satisfying. *This is the way work is supposed to be*, I thought.

My work, on the other hand, felt unsatisfying and unfinished, at least lately. I measured most sessions by the clock, not by the progress we made. In fact, I almost always ended by saying, "We'll pick it up here next time you come in." Not that there weren't breakthroughs—there were—but rarely did things ever come to a clear ending point. With so much brokenness in the world, I felt like the work was never finished.

For a moment I looked at Josh working a long wooden beam through the saw, and my eyes filled with tears as I remembered his words from the cross: "*It is finished.*" For the first time I realized that in that moment he must have had a deep sense of satisfaction knowing that he did his work really well.

That's what's been missing in my work lately, I thought. What I wanted, what I needed was to hear someone say, "You did a good job. Well done. I'm proud of you." In that moment it was so clear. We were created with a purpose. Each of us has a job to do. Work is an integral part of life, and it always has been. Right at the beginning Adam was put in the Garden and told to work it, and we've been working it ever since.

Could it be? Was that it? Had Josh been trying to tell me all day that our work will never really be done, not even here?

Nothing satisfies the soul like feeling we've accomplished something.

The idea that people worked in heaven took me by surprise. For some reason I'd thought that heaven was like retirement—nothing to do, and plenty of time to do it. But now that I thought about it, it made perfect sense. We're all made in God's image, after all. And like him, we've all been given the ability to create. Besides, nothing satisfies the soul like feeling we've accomplished something.

"I am so very proud of you," Josh said. "You're finally beginning to put some of the pieces together on your own. It's that kind of thinking that's needed if we're going to be delivered from evil and put an end to the conspiracy once and for all."

I was about to ask him what he meant by that when he raised his index finger to his lips, shook his head, and said, "Now's not the time for more information. Now is the time for you to unpack and reprocess what you already know. Understanding comes slowly, in bits and pieces. One thing builds upon another. Too much too soon will only confuse you. Trust me, it will all be clear to you when you're ready. Besides, right now we've got work to do."

The sawmill was an old building made of barn wood, and the sunlight streaked in between the slats. The floor was covered with dirt and sawdust. At one end was a pile of newly cut logs in ten-foot lengths. Josh had a pencil on his ear and a list in his pocket, and he knew exactly how many pieces of each length he wanted. We measured and cut the boards to the lengths written on Josh's lumber list, and by mid-afternoon we had worked our way through several piles of lumber of various sizes. We had one-by-fours, two-by-fours, four-by-fours, two-by-sixes, and two-by-tens each separated and stacked in racks by size. The last stack of boards we had to cut were two-by-tens that were twelve feet long. They each needed to be trimmed to eleven feet seven inches. I measured and marked each board, and Josh cut them to size, but when we got down to the last board I discovered that it was three inches short.

"Do you want me to go get another two-by-ten out of the stacks?" I asked.

"No," Josh said. "That's all right, we'll make do with this one." Then he grabbed the board firmly with both hands and stretched it lengthwise like it was made of Play-Doh. When he handed it to me, I placed it on the pile with the others, and it was exactly eleven feet seven inches.

"There," he said. "I think that's enough for today. I don't know about you, but I could use something to drink." The two of us were both hot and sweaty and covered in sawdust, and as we walked over to an old pump in the corner of the barn, Josh motioned to a row of cups on the wall. I found my name neatly lettered on one.

"Grab mine too, will ya?" Josh asked. And I did. We took turns pumping and drinking, and the lumber list fell out of his pocket and onto the dirt floor. As he picked it up I couldn't help but notice what it said at the top of the list.

"Excuse me, Josh," I said kind of sheepishly. "But I think that piece of paper in your pocket has my last name on it."

"You're right," Josh replied. "It does. Does that surprise you? But you're not the only Hunt in the world, you know. Besides, I've always been very clear about this. When I left, I said that I was going to prepare a place for you. At the time, of course, the 'you' was plural, but for anyone who answers when I knock on the door of their heart, it becomes singular, a personal promise between us. And I always make good on my promises."

"You're not planning on making good on that promise to me anytime soon, are you?"

"It's always sooner than anyone thinks," he said. "But not now, not today, anyway. That day will come when you least expect it, like a thief in the night."

Thinking about one's own demise is always sobering, and as I sat and contemplated the gravity of his words, I thought how my death might impact the people I loved the most. I wanted to ask for more time, because they're not ready yet. To be honest, *I'm* not ready yet, and that's when I saw it: half buried in the sawdust was a little blue baseball cap with the name "Ben" stitched above the bill.

"That's Ben's hat!" I said excitedly.

"You're right," Josh replied. "He lost it the summer he was seven when the two of you walked up here looking for pirate treasure."

Memories came flooding back. One cloudy day in July, we packed a couple of peanut butter sandwiches and went exploring. Ben loved adventure, and he and I would often take a hike just to see what we could see. That day he wanted to pretend we were pirates looking for lost gold. When we found that abandoned sawmill, it became our pirate ship for the afternoon.

We climbed up into the loft, swung on a rope that hung from the rafters, and made swords out of some one-bys. I was chasing Ben around, and as he tried to scamper up the ladder, he slipped and fell into the pile of sawdust. It knocked the wind out of him, and for a minute I thought he was really hurt bad. I was relieved when he caught his breath and started crying, but when I walked him back home my mother wasn't very happy with me.

"Where have you boys been?" she asked. "And why is Ben crying?"

Ben told her how he fell off a ladder in an old sawmill, and then she was all over me.

"You're supposed to be keeping an eye on him, Sky," she said in a reprimanding tone. "What were you doing in a sawmill? Ben could have been killed or something. I swear, sometimes I wonder what you're thinking. If you can't keep out of trouble, then maybe you boys better stick around the cottage."

That afternoon we had to stay inside and play Monopoly with my sister, which to two adventurous boys was just a waste of good daylight.

That night I said to Ben, "If you want to hang with the big boys, there's going to be no crying! Do you understand?"

He nodded that he did, and as far as I knew, Ben never cried again.

Then it hit me. Here I was spending the day with Jesus, and I was lost on a trip down memory lane. What was I thinking? I was about to apologize to him like I do sometimes when my mind starts wandering while I'm praying, but he spoke before I could.

"We worked right through lunch. I don't know what I was thinking! I'm supposed to be keeping an eye on you. I better get you back before your supper company gets here."

As we walked back down the hill, I said, "Josh, I have so many unanswered questions."

"I know," he replied. "But you've just got to be patient. Answers take time. Wisdom takes endurance."

After that, he put his hand on my shoulder, and we walked in silence.

encouragement

Bart, having never received any words of encouragement myself, I'm not sure how they're
supposed to sound. But here goes: I believe
in you.

Lisa Simpson

5

I was getting dressed when I noticed it: A two-tone, blue metallic '57 Chevy Bel Air was parking alongside the cottage. As I watched, I realized that Florence Kowalski was inside.

I couldn't believe my eyes. "Florence!" I shouted from the open window. "Is that really you?"

She waved, and I ran down the stairs and out the door to greet her.

Florence stood outside the passenger side door with her arms open, ready to greet me.

"Just look at you," she said, hugging me as though it were perfectly normal for dead friends to come calling in the late afternoon. "Aren't you the handsome one? You look so much like your mother. Of course, you always did. I can't believe it . . . little Schuyler Hunt all grown up, and a doctor too. She's so proud of you."

Florence looked like I had always remembered: wispy thin with platinum blonde hair, wearing a black-and-white polka-dot blouse, red pedal pushers, and a pair of sassy red high-heeled shoes.

She was my mother's oldest and closest friend, and when she died, a part of Mom died too. But a part of her also lived on in Mom's memory and heart. They'd known each other since grade school, and Florence's husband, Ray, grew up near Dad on College Avenue. In fact, they were the ones who set my parents up on a blind date. Dad was tall, cocky, athletic, and handsome, and Mom was beautiful but quiet. Dad always said he married up. But their families differed, and their romance almost ended before it started.

When someone we love dies, a part of us dies too, but a part of them also lives on in us.

Grandpa Jacobs was the vice president of Jansma's Dairy, which meant that they lived well, and when it came to religion, he was old school. He and Grandma went to church twice on Sunday, and they also were regulars in Sunday school and the Wednesday night prayer meeting. They were Scofield Bible teetotalers who were loving but stern. The only time I ever got a licking with a belt was over Grandpa's knee. I learned real quickly that you didn't sass Grandma in front of Grandpa.

Grandpa's world was very black and white. You either played on the side of good or on the side of evil, and there was no middle ground. "We're living in the last days," he'd say, and he believed it. He fully expected that without so much as a moment's notice, Gabriel would blow his trumpet, the clouds would part, and the final Judge would come and separate the sheep from the goats, which meant that we all needed to be ready.

What we believe ought to be visible in the way we live our lives.

As far as Grandpa was concerned, that meant that what you believed ought to be visible in the way you lived your life. Ten cents of every dollar he made went back in the collection bag on Sunday, and if someone knocked on their back door looking for a handout, they got one. "You never know when you might be entertaining angels," Grandma would say. I never saw any angels, but there was often an unexpected guest at their dinner table.

Grandpa and Grandma lived only a few blocks from the freight yard, and during the Great Depression a lot of people rode the rails. Each of them was in as bad a shape as the last, and eventually the word spread around the hobo campfire that if you were hungry, Mrs. Jacobs would always share their supper with you. But be warned, because she'd also share her mind and her gospel along with her goulash.

In fact, Grandma was such an easy mark that the hobos took a piece of coal and put an X on the curb in front of their house. Sometimes the rain would wash it off, and then when Grandpa would pull his big gray Hudson Terraplane in front of the house, he'd have to go downstairs into the coal bin to get a piece of charcoal so he could put that X back on the curb. "God has blessed me to be a blessing to others," he'd say, and he meant it.

God has blessed us to be a blessing to others.

Grandpa Hunt, on the other hand, was an unemployed wallpaper hanger who had a taste for whiskey and White Owl cigars. He smoked White Owls for so long that he began to look like one, with black round-rim glasses, a weathered red beak of a nose, and bushy, feathered eyebrows. He bought the cigars at the corner store, three for a nickel, and he made whiskey out of potatoes in a still in the basement. Later in life, he switched to Kessler's, but he made do with home brew during Prohibition.

His idea of being a regular at church was attending every Christmas and Easter (unless someone called and wanted to go rabbit hunting—then all bets were off). Just about every Sunday, Grandpa's knee would start to hurt something awful right after breakfast, and as much as he wanted to go to church, he'd send Grandma and the kids on without him. They didn't have a car, and it was too far for him to walk, what with his bad knee and all. The way he saw it, if God really wanted him in church, he'd have made sure they had a car. Besides, the sermon was the same every Sunday. "All that preacher wants," Grandpa would say, "is to meddle in your business and get into your wallet."

Grandpa Hunt had a little chip on his shoulder about how his life turned out. He didn't think he got a fair shake. He felt that working for the WPA for side pork and a loaf of bread was beneath him. Every day he would have to walk downtown, stand in line, and then catch a wagon to whatever work site the government had for him that day.

Grandpa only had an eighth grade education, but he was a skilled craftsman who could work with wood, metal, and plaster. He also grew up around horses and had a way with them, but most days he'd end up working on a crew that was building roads out of paving bricks for the rich people. Every day Grandpa would tell the foreman that he was a skilled tradesman and that laying paving bricks was a waste of his talent and the government's money, but the foreman wouldn't listen.

Eventually Grandpa stopped talking with the foreman, and every time he'd get a mind to, he'd take a little nip of potato whiskey from the flask in his pocket and keep laying those pavers. The depression was hard on Grandpa, and he in turn made it hard on everyone else—everyone, that is, but me.

For some reason he liked me. He'd come by school and tell the teacher that I had a dentist or doctor appointment and then take me fishing. I'd row while he'd talk about people like Johnny Bosma and Jack Rietsma and how they'd get into it with the west-siders, and then they'd all go have a beer. You see, the Polish section of town was on the west side of the river that divided the city, and in those days there was bad blood between the Dutch Protestants and the Polish Catholics. Prejudice ran deep on both sides, and sometimes it was fueled by the clergy. Neither group wanted one of their flock to marry "one of them," and it was the subject of many a sermon.

Both congregations were made up of poor, uneducated immigrants who competed for the entry-level jobs in the local fur-niture factories, and jobs were scarce. To hear Grandpa tell it, the west-siders were a little lower in the pecking order than he was. So naturally, whenever one of them got a job ahead of him, he felt like they were taking food off of his table.

Every time it happened, Grandpa and his boys would go out at night stinking for a fight, and the west-siders were more than happy to give it to them. Like Grandma used to say, "Grandpa would splash on his bitterness like cologne, and anyone who got close to him could smell it."

Once he said to me, "The trick to life is to take what you can get, and then figure out a way to keep it." I smoked my first cigar in a boat with him, and I had my first taste of whiskey from his flask too. I choked on both, and when I said that it tasted like kerosene, he said he'd bring me a Nehi soda next time, which he did. Grandpa kept his eye on the time, and he'd drop me off back at school before my bus left at 3:15. He'd always warn me not to tell my mother about our outings, and of course I didn't.

I was always a little afraid of Grandpa, but at the same time, I liked him. One day when I was about ten, he was doing some painting at our house and I wanted to help. Grandpa was very particular and wasn't about to let me help, so he took an empty paint can and filled it with water, climbed up the ladder in the garage, and pressed the can against the ceiling. Then he took a broom handle and stuck it underneath the can and told me to hold it. Then he took the ladder and went inside.

I stood there holding that broom handle, pressing the can against the ceiling, until my arms were aching. Finally I yelled, "Grandpa, I can't hold this much longer. I need your help."

"No, you don't," he yelled back.

"Yes, I do," I shouted.

"Listen, boy, I don't want to help you, and I don't want you to help me, have you got that?"

"But Grandpa," I protested, "if you don't help me, this can of water is going to come crashing down and I'm going to get all wet!"

"A smart boy would let go of that stick and run as fast as he could," he said. "And then he'd go play someplace else."

And as that can of water came crashing down, that's exactly what I did.

As a kid, I really liked going to Grandpa Hunt's after church on Sunday. There you could ride a bike, throw a football, pound a nail into something, or play cards with the grown-ups, and you never had to go to church again at night. Besides, as tough as Grandpa was, Grandma was as kind and as gentle a soul as ever walked the earth, and consequently, there was always a lot of laughing at their house, even on Sunday.

As you can imagine, there was a clash of cultures when Mom and Dad first started dating. My mother thought the Hunts were a little wicked, and my dad thought the Jacobs family was wrapped a little too tight—but somehow, they took bits and pieces from both sides and built a life for themselves. Life is a matter of learning how to take the best from the people you love and letting go of the rest.

Life is a matter of learning how to take the best from the people you love and letting go of the rest.

Ray was the best man at my parents' wedding, and Florence was the maid of honor. My folks returned the favor for them a few months later. They were as close as any two couples could be. Dad and Ray joined the Navy when World War II broke out two years later, and Mom and Florence got an apartment together. After the war, the four of them lived together in a tiny apartment until they got on their feet financially.

Both Dad and Ray served an apprenticeship as tool and die makers, and they later changed from building dies to designing them. As tool engineers, they made a good living, but growing up, I always thought the Kowalskis were a little above us.

Ray had a good job at a furniture company, and it showed in their lifestyle. They lived well. My dad, on the other hand, went into business for himself, and the early years were lean. One year, for example, I remember Florence and Ray's oldest boys, Ron and Tom, each got a brand-new three-speed bike with those skinny racing tires. I had to share an old, fat-wheeled girls' bike with my sister. Ron and Tom went to East High in the suburbs, while Sharon, Ben, and I went to Ottawa Hills in the inner city. They always had the latest style of clothes, and I always got their hand-me-downs with patches on the knees. Each year Ron, Tom, Sharon, and I would go downtown and get our picture taken with the department store Santa Claus. Year after year, I'd have on the coat that Ron or Tom wore in the picture the year before. Ben was five years younger than me, so all the hand-me-downs had made their way to the mission by the time he came along.

I guess I always felt a little inferior to the Kowalski boys, but if they felt superior to me, it never showed. They always let me tag along with them wherever they went, and if someone asked who the squirt was on the girls' bike, they'd say, "This is our friend, Sky," and it would be all right. I looked up to them, but they didn't look down on me. Like their mother, they were always gracious. I guess that's why I didn't really mind when Ben tagged along with me. What goes around comes around, and what I got from Ron and Tom, I tried to give to Ben.

Ron and Tom were the coolest guys I knew. They played baseball and basketball, and in high school, Ron ran cross-country and Tom played football. For several years, Ron held the state record in the mile and the two-mile run, and Tom was an all-conference football player. Ron won a full-ride scholarship to Michigan, and the next year Tom went to Michigan State on a football scholarship. They were in the limelight, and I stood in their shadow.

Our families remained close throughout the years. When Ray died, his kids asked me to say a few words. Of course I agreed, but for some reason their minister felt threatened by that. When he found out I wasn't from his particular denominational tribe, he prohibited me from participating. I tried to assure him that I didn't know anything about denominations, and I certainly wasn't going to talk about any of that, but it didn't matter. His mind was made up.

I don't think I ever thought about it before, but I don't think God ever intended for there to be denominations. Satan drew those lines. He's the master of divide and conquer, and history is full of examples of that. Wars and rumors of wars have too often been about religion, and it breaks God's heart. He said we should love one another, not argue with one another, and never is that more true than when someone has lost a person they love.

In the end, Ron decided to make the service more of a memorial, and a few of us shared our memories of his dad. To be honest, it was as holy as any service I'd ever been to, and nobody seemed to miss the liturgical stuff. "That's not who my folks were," Ron said. "They always included, not excluded." And he was right—that was who they were, especially Florence. She had a way of looking after stray cats, and kids, and frightened baby birds. And to me, she was my other mother.

Everyone always welcomes a word of encouragement.

Florence was what some people call "a Barnabas," an encourager—someone who always found some way to make you feel better about yourself. Everyone always welcomes a word of encouragement, and I was no exception.

When Ron ran in the Olympics in 1968 and no one could talk about anything else, she praised my performance in the senior class play. She said that I was remarkable. I wasn't, but I needed to hear that then.

When Tom went off to football camp for the Detroit Lions and everyone was saying what a tremendous future he had, Florence said that she thought it was simply fantastic that I played guitar in the Ya Ha Whoopee Band. I needed to hear that too.

Perhaps most of all, I remember when Tom died. He suffered an aneurism the next season in training camp. He was young and full of life, with so much to live for. None of us were ready to say good-bye.

No mother should ever have to stand beside the casket of her child. I went to the funeral home hoping somehow to help her, to be strong for her, to say something encouraging to her, but when I saw Tom lying there, I lost it. Florence did what only Florence would do. She put away her grief, put her arm around me, and said, "It'll be all right, it'll be all right. Tom is with Jesus now."

But instead of making me feel better, her words made me feel worse. Before that, I thought I knew who God was and how things were supposed to work. He was the superintendent of the universe, and it was his job to make sure that things like this didn't happen. Young people weren't supposed to die—that was part of the bargain. Good was stronger than evil. That's what I'd been taught, so even then, I half expected God to swoop in at the last minute and miraculously make things right.

Sure, we might have to temporarily go through some difficult times, but in the end, the scales would be balanced, we'd learn our lesson, and everything would work out fine. Life was supposed to be fair, at least for those of us who believed in Jesus and tried to live a good life.

But God didn't swoop, and we were left to deal with the cold reality that life wasn't fair. To be honest, I was surprised, hurt, angry, disappointed, and a little scared. After all, if Tom's life could just be snuffed out like a candle in the wind, then none of us were safe. Then evil really was random. Then bad things happened willy-nilly, with no rhyme or reason, and no matter how hard we tried, none of us could make sense of it.

Of course, now as an adult, I've learned to take a longer view of such things. I understand that God never promised that life would be fair. He just promised that he'd be there when it wasn't. It took me a long time to figure that out after the accident. I'm still trying to figure it out in some ways, I guess. But now as much as I can, I try to live by faith, not by sight. I trust that such random acts of evil will all be worked out by God *someday*. Someday, the scales will be balanced. Someday, we'll learn our lesson, and things will work out fine. Someday, we'll see things from God's perspective and everything will make perfect sense.

God never promised that life would be fair. He just promised to be there when it wasn't.

But having said that, even now, death and tragedy still catch me off guard, and then doubt comes calling once again. I lay staring at the ceiling in the middle of the night, and I question. "Why, God?" I ask, and to be honest, sometimes hurt, anger, disappointment, and fear smother my faith with a pillow.

"Is Tom with you?" I asked.

"No," Florence replied. "He and Ray already had plans to go fishing out at Promise Point, but they said to say hi. You boys can catch up next time—you'll have an eternity to do that, but this is my time and I didn't want to share it. Is that okay?"

"Sure, that's fine with me!" And it was.

We went inside and Florence cooked while we talked, mostly about our families, and time sort of got away from us.

"How's Sharon?" she asked. "And Ben? Is everything all right with him?"

"Sharon's great, and Ben is doing okay too," I replied, not wanting to disappoint her.

"Oh, good. I always knew you'd look after him."

Her words sort of rubbed salt in my already guilty conscience, but I smiled and nodded as if she were right.

We sat down in the dining room, I said grace, simple and quick, and then we ate. Florence's dinner was comfort food: fruit salad with coconut, bananas, marshmallows, and mandarin oranges;

smoked sausage; and macaroni and cheese—not the stuff out of a box but the real deal. She used aged cheddar, Dutch gouda, baby Swiss, and Stilton bleu crumbles, with Parmigiano-Reggiano toasted bread crumbs on top.

After dessert of French silk chocolate cream pie, Florence stood up and said, "I'm sorry, but I've got to get going. I promised to pick up Davie, and he'll be waiting."

Davie had lived hard and died young, and Florence was just as happy to have him close. Two of her four children were with her and Ray in heaven now.

We said our good-byes as Florence cut me an extra piece of pie for later. As she wrapped the rest of the pie in aluminum foil, she said, "If it's okay, I'm going to take some pie home to the boys. Davie might want a piece later."

"Of course," I replied. "Please take it. I'm sure someone else will be by with more food tomorrow."

"That's right," Florence said. "That's the way it works." She turned to go.

"Wait! Don't you have something for me?"

"Oh my, yes," she said. "I almost forgot! *Never miss the chance to make someone feel better.* Nothing combats the conspiracy like kindness. It's really the heart of Christianity. It muffles the drums of war, soothes the worried mind, strengthens the feeblest knees, and restores our faith in the human race. Yes, if you want to change people, you've got to start by changing their conditions. And Sky, if you see Ron and Nancy, tell them how proud of them I am, will you?"

Nancy was Florence's baby, the youngest of her four children. I hadn't seen her since Ray's funeral, but the mention of her name made me think how much she looked like Florence.

"I will," I said. "I promise."

Florence put both hands on my cheeks and kissed me good-bye.

"Scout," she said, "when you were little, you were always tagging along behind, but looking at you now, I can see that somewhere along the way you got out ahead. You're leading the way. It's up to you now. So don't let us down on this."

I wanted to ask her what she meant by that, but before I could, she turned and got into the car and drove away. It felt like maybe she was talking about Ben; then again, maybe it was just me. He'd been on my mind since I got here, and sooner or later, I was going to have to unload my thoughts on someone—but it didn't feel quite right with Florence. I ate the second piece of silk pie, said a prayer thanking God that he'd put Florence in my life, and went off to bed with a full belly and a soul full of questions.

Never miss the chance to make someone else's life better.

priorities

The key is not to prioritize what's on your schedule, but to schedule your priorities.

Stephen R. Covey

6

The next morning, I got up early and walked down to the lake. The wind had kicked up, and the sound of the waves lapping against the aluminum boat lulled me into the memory of other peaceful days. I remembered being here as a kid, or at least someplace that looked like this. My parents rented a cottage for a month, and it seemed like each day was better than the last. Every morning I'd wake up and go fishing or swimming or sailing or exploring. At the time I didn't realize how special it was.

My dad worked three of the four weeks, driving the two-hour commute on weekends and also on Wednesday night. When he was gone, I was in charge—at least that's what he'd tell me every time he left—and I took every opportunity to rub my sister's nose in it.

I was the oldest boy, the firstborn son, and those were more chauvinistic days. Ben was happy to tag along behind. He looked up to me, and there was never any doubt in his mind that I was in charge.

I guess that's why when the tragedy fell on Ben, some of it fell on me too. We both carry scars from that day. His are physical and mine are emotional, and even now when I think about it, my first instinct is to run away and hide. A part of me has been running away from that day ever since, but no matter how hard I try, I've never really been able to hide. The memory dogs my tracks like a bloodhound.

I must have sat there on that dock, lost in thought, for several hours. I was thinking about what it would be like to stay here or to go home and feeling torn between the two.

With the blowing wind, I barely heard the voice behind me. "You missed breakfast, so I packed us a little lunch."

When I turned around, a slender brunette in her thirties stood on the shore.

"Ahbee asked me to spend some time with you today," she said. "My name is Ru-ah, but you can call me Rae."

Rae had chestnut hair highlighted by blonde streaks, and her freckles spoke to her love of the sun. Her hair fell to her shoulders and then swept up and back as if the wind had just blown it off her face. Rae was wearing a sleeveless black blouse that buttoned up the front in a V, a khaki pencil skirt, and open-toed Dr. Scholl's sandals that clomped as she walked out to meet me on the dock. Her earrings and her eyes were pale green, and both seemed to sparkle in the sunlight. Even in those sandals, she seemed to dance as she walked.

She brushed up beside me, and for a moment I felt a little flushed and awkward. There was something earthy and yet innocent about her, and I wondered if she knew just how beautiful she was.

"Come on," she said, motioning with her head. "Let's you and I take a little walk."

We went down the same two-track that Roz and I had driven the other night, but in the daylight I noticed that it was lined with cottages, big and small, in a variety of colors, all kept neat and tidy. "Who lives in these?" I asked.

"Different people at different times," Rae replied.

There was something very familiar about her, but I couldn't quite put my finger on it.

"May I ask you a question?" I asked.

"Sure."

"Who are you?"

"Who do you think I am?" she responded.

I was beginning to get frustrated with the mystery and double-talk. "No, really," I said. "I want to know."

"I think you already know."

"Humor me," I said.

"All right. I am who you think I am. The children of Israel called me Ru-ah, the breath, the wind, the one who hovered over the chaos before time began. Josh's disciples called me the Pneuma, the Spirit, the unseen force, the one he sent to be your constant companion. The prophets called me Wisdom, the inspiration for your best thoughts and your deepest passion, and they were all right. When you feel something but don't see anything—particularly something calming, comforting, inspiring, or loving—it's me . . . it's always me. I am your constant companion. I am the peace of mind that Joshua left behind."

As she spoke I began to see the family resemblance. The crinkle in her nose when she smiled, the twinkle in her eye, the sound of her laugh—it was all so much like Ahbee.

"There is so much more to the business of life and death than you allow yourself to believe," she continued. "So much more than you can see, or touch, or taste, or hear. Yet, for some reason, you all seem to buy into the conspiracy that Christianity can be reduced to creeds and confessions and the questions and answers in the catechism. You want a handful of easily understood words. But words are insufficient. Can you see that?"

Before I could answer, Rae went on. "Perhaps the best thing I can do is reduce it to one word. If you want it in words, then I am 'Love.' And tell me, if you can, who can describe such a thing? If you need more of an explanation, I will try, but like

I warned you, it will take a lot of words. Poets and musicians have put pen to paper for as long as words have been written, and none of them have done it justice. Sometimes little flashes of truth dash across the page, but even then they can only know in part, not the whole.

"Love, as they say, is a mystery, and I am the love of God that's whispered in every beat of your heart; the love that speaks in the soundless silence of immortal, invisible things that are forever happening all around you; the love that's muffled in the rustling leaves of the trees and hidden in the cool breeze that blows off the lake in the early morning. I am all around you, and yet deep within you."

There is so much more to life than we can see, or touch, or taste, or hear.

"You're getting a little deep there, aren't you, Rae?" I said. "I'm not sure I really understood much of what you just said. Is there a way you could come right out and say it in simple terms?"

"Simple isn't always as simple as it sounds," she said. "In the ancient words of faith, truth was tied up in a neat and tidy bundle, so that you could carry it around with you wherever you went, and I am a part of that. You all say it—'I believe in the Holy Spirit'—but you never stop and let the words sink in. You can know *what* you believe in, but *who* you believe in will always be somewhat of a mystery.

"Now here is the secret to understanding," Rae continued. "The more you understand *what* you believe, the more it should affect the way you live your life, and the more it affects the way you live, the more you'll understand the mystery of *who* I am. Does that make sense? Do you understand what I'm saying?" she asked.

I looked up, but before I could answer, Rae went on. "No, of course you don't. It's the handicap of humanity, the price tag of sin, the downfall of Adam and those who follow after him. In your desire to understand both good and evil, you have become so tainted by evil that you can no longer totally understand good. But in spite of that, God loves you. It is what you confess in your creeds. The love of God, his Holy Spirit, is your constant companion. I am with you always, and knowing that should give you great comfort and drastically affect the way you live.

The more we understand what we believe, the more it should affect the way we live.

"Unfortunately, it all too often doesn't. Instead of resting in that, you quickly move on to the rest—'the holy catholic church, the communion of saints, the forgiveness of sins, the resurrection of the body, and the life everlasting'—and these things also can too easily become part of the conspiracy because they're shrouded in mystery. Like everyone else, you desperately want eternal life, but for some reason, you choose each day to waste the life you have. You fill the days of this life with things that won't matter much in the next."

"There you go again," I said. "I don't get it. You've got to give me something a little more concrete. An example of some kind."

"Okay, take gold, for example," Rae said. "When John wrote that the streets of heaven were paved in gold, he didn't mean that it was there for the taking, but for the leaving—that it would be as worthless as the dirt on your shoes. The only thing that has value here is love. That's the currency of heaven. That's the pearl of great price. Even though it costs you nothing, that's the world's most priceless treasure: God's love for you, your love for God, and your love for each other.

"Knowing and understanding that, if you want to invest in something eternal, you need to invest your life in people. That's what you were created to do: to love God and to love each other. And when you fail to do that, there is this restless spirit deep down in your soul, and that restlessness is me. I refuse to let you settle for anything less.

"Oh, at times, like when you look at the face of a newborn

baby, when you dance with your wife on your fiftieth anniversary, when you gather around the table at Thanksgiving and get too choked up to pray—at times like that you're not far from it, not far from the kingdom. But for the most part, you're just too busy to listen to the whispered hush of the Holy Spirit, and so the love of God slips through your fingers like sand."

For a few moments we walked along in silence. The only sounds were my feet sloshing through the puddles in the path and a bullfrog somewhere off in the distance. When he fell silent, I turned and looked at Rae with a wrinkled brow.

"Does that help you?" Rae finally asked.

"Some," I said. "I didn't get it all, but some. So what you're saying is that I've let things get turned around in my life? I've devalued the things that matter most and inflated the things that matter least?"

Too often we devalue the things that matter most and inflate the things that matter least.

"You understand more than you realize. And the guilt," she continued. "There is a point when you have to let go of the guilt, Scout. It wasn't really your fault anyway, and in time, I hope you can come to see that."

I wanted to walk and talk some more because I wondered if Rae was talking about what I *thought* she was talking about. But Rae motioned to the lodge and said, "That's enough for one day. Besides, there's someone waiting for you."

I had been so caught up in our conversation that I didn't realize we had turned back. Evidently we had headed back toward the cottage sometime during our walk. That's when I saw it. There were several puddles in the road, and I had been trying to walk around them, but Rae never altered her step. And here's the strange thing: I noticed that she was walking on the puddles, not in them. It was as if for the briefest of moments the water was frozen under her feet.

"That's a pretty neat trick," I said, pointing toward the puddle.

"I learned that from Josh," she said.

"I should have known," I said, and we kept walking. The sun began to sink over the sand dune to the west, and knowing how things worked around here, I looked up the driveway to see who might have come to visit.

In the driveway sat a white '77 Volkswagen Rabbit Wolfsburg Edition with a red scotch plaid interior. I recognized it immediately. I spent ten years in the car business before going back to grad school, and I remembered selling it. There was nothing all that special about the car, but there was something very special about the woman who drove it.

"Mom?" I shouted, running toward her open arms.

"Sky!" she whispered, and I burst into tears.

There's something powerful about hearing your mother say your name, and when she wrapped her arms around me, I felt like a little boy again. Her long, dangling earrings brushed against my neck as I held her, and I caught a faint whisper of her Chanel No. 5 perfume. This was what I was most homesick for, and for the first time in a long time, my heart was home again.

"This is your house, isn't it, Mom? I knew it as soon as I saw it. It's so much like that cottage we rented when I was a kid that every room floods my mind with warm memories."

"Sorry to disappoint you, Sky," she said. "But this is the guest cottage. It's here for people like you. My place isn't quite finished yet; in fact, we just finalized the blueprints. I'm excited to watch them start construction, but I'm in no hurry. Right now I'm staying with Herb and Gerry, and that's nice. It's giving us a chance to catch up."

That's when I realized that what made me feel at home was being with her again.

She was born Audrey Rae to John and Esther Jacobs, and because of her loving heart and generous spirit, we gave our daughter Kelly her middle name. I was one of the lucky ones in life. My mom and dad had always loved me unconditionally, and she had proven it again and again. Growing up, I'd disappointed her more times than I'd care to count.

Once she was mad at me about something (probably for hitting my sister), and she sent me to my room.

"Don't come out until you're ready to apologize," she said as I slammed my bedroom door. I knew the drill—this was not the first time I'd been sent to my room, and I also knew that if I came out too quickly, the apology wouldn't be accepted.

"You better go back there and think about what you've done, mister," she'd say, and her tone let me know that I'd be there for a while.

Having the attention span of a Labrador puppy at the time, I decided to use my jackknife to carefully cut my way through the left lower edge of the screen in my bedroom and then sneak outside to play. About an hour later, I jumped up, grabbed the outside sill of my bedroom window, pulled myself up and in, and folded the screen back as close to normal as I could. Then I walked out into the living room, apologized, and went back outside to play.

The next week, she was washing windows, and she discovered that the screen had been cut. Thinking that her son would never do anything that stupid, she naturally assumed that someone was trying to get into the house, not out. She worried all afternoon about the screen-cutting bandit until my dad came home and heard what happened.

Dad knew my dark soul much better than my mom. He took me into the bedroom and talked to me about the importance of being honest. After several denials, I finally admitted the truth, and he made me go apologize to my mother.

There's something awful about disappointing your mother, and for me, the worst part was that she cried. Well, when she cried, I cried, and a few minutes later, she was holding me and I kept repeating, "I'm sorry, Mom, I'm sorry."

She said, "I forgive you, Sky, I forgive you!"

The last few years of Mom's life had been difficult. She had osteoporosis, diabetes, and complications from sixty-some years of cigarettes, and it had robbed her of the joy of life. She lost feeling in her feet, was tethered to an oxygen bottle, and took a regimen of pills morning, noon, and night. She could no longer do the things she'd always done, and when anyone else tried to do them for her, it made her feel useless.

Mom was a giver, not a taker, and being forced to be on the receiving end of things was a bitter pill for her to swallow. People who are used to giving sometimes have a hard time receiving. At times she'd take her frustration out on those she loved, and in the last few years of her life, I didn't visit as often as she would have liked. I let the busyness of my life reduce our relationship to phone calls and cards. For

> *People who are used to giving sometimes have a hard time receiving.*

some reason I found it easier to say "I love you" with a pen than in person. I'd see her on holidays and stop by for a few minutes when I was in town, but not like I used to. She never complained, but I knew it bothered her.

"I'm sorry, Mom," I said as we held each other in the driveway. "I'm so sorry."

"For what?" she asked, with a puzzled look on her face.

"For everything. For the way I let you down, for all the times I made you worry or broke your heart. But mostly for not coming to see you as much as I should have," I said, taking a long, deep breath.

"Nonsense! You came when you could. You had your girls to look after and your practice, and I know how much time you spend looking out for Ben these days. So don't be ridiculous. You've got nothing to be sorry about! We were always connected at the heart."

As always, hearing her say that I was forgiven made me feel

better. God always stands at the end of the driveway of heaven ready to welcome the prodigals home, and Mom stood right beside him. She always said God's not about guilt or blame; that's who *we* are, not who he is.

"Come on," she said. "Let's go inside, and you can get washed up. But don't dawdle . . . dinner's almost ready. And don't forget to use soap!"

I did as I was told, and when I came down, the dining room table was set and so was she. The tablecloth beneath the gold-rimmed china had once been her mother's, and silverware, not stainless, sat atop pale green linen napkins. Clear goblets were filled with water, ice, and a slice of lemon, and a wine glass bubbled with something that sparkled. A turkey, browned and sliced, sat on a silver tray surrounded by bowls of riced potatoes, corn, green bean casserole, cranberry relish with orange peel, and dressing. Mom always made Aunt Mina's duck dressing. It was an old family recipe made with sausage and celery, and it was my favorite.

God always stands at the end of the driveway of heaven ready to welcome the prodigals home.

When I first walked into the dining room, Mom was wearing a green flowered apron that hung from her neck and was tied around her waist, but she took it off for dinner. Beneath the apron she wore a cream-colored pearl-button blouse, a pearl necklace and bracelet, a peach-colored suit, and black-and-cream checked high-heeled shoes. Like my wife, Mom had always had a weakness for shoes, and Dad had always had a weakness for Mom. He always said she was beautiful, and he was right.

We talked and laughed and talked some more, mostly about me and the struggles of growing up. She and I had spent many nights sitting at our kitchen table struggling with math, geography, or reading.

"Read the sentence out loud," she'd say. "Come on, you can do it. Sound it out."

"I fa, I fa, I fa, I fed the god."

"No," she'd say. "You didn't feed God, you fed the *dog*. Come on, Scout, you've got to think. Now try the next sentence."

"I sa, I sa, I was the cat."

"Come on now, you weren't the cat. You *saw* the cat."

"No, I didn't," I'd say in frustration.

"It's all right," she'd say. "That's enough for tonight. We'll try it again tomorrow."

Unlike those nights that seemed to last forever, this one flew by. "I must be going," she said. "But before I do, I've got something to show you."

She pulled a piece of paper and a pen out of her purse and began to draw circles. The first one was ever so tiny. The next one was a little larger and encased the smaller one. She kept drawing circles until they ran off the page.

Then she said to me, "In this little circle, there's just enough room for you and God. That's it, no one else. In the next circle, there is room for you and your girls. Just enough room for the people you love the most."

"And you," I said. "You'd be in that circle too."

"That's so sweet," she said. "But no. I'd probably be in the third circle, along with Ben and Sharon and your dad. In the next circle

If you were going to draw the circles of life, who'd be closest to the center?

you can put the other people you love, and in the next one, your closest friends. The circles keep going out and eventually, when you get past friends and neighbors and coworkers, the circles are filled with people you don't know. It's not that you don't care about what happens to those people, it's just that you care more about the people closest to the center. Do you understand?" she asked.

"Of course," I replied, wondering what the point was.

"Now here's the point," Mom said as though she was reading my thoughts. "We tend to live our lives several circles out. We work, or go to school, or spend our free time with people in those circles, and we spend our lives worrying about what they think. What we wear, what we drive, where we live, all of these things are outer circle stuff. Do you understand?"

"Not really."

"Let me try to explain," she said. "Imagine that you just got a new car, and on your way home you saw your neighbor. What would you do?"

"I don't know. I'd probably honk and wave and roll down the window and say hi."

"Exactly," she said. "And you would because you'd hope he would think the car was cool, right?"

"Yeah, I guess so."

"But now, here's the thing. When you got home, do you think Carol would love you more because you got that new car?"

"Of course not," I said.

"And yet," she continued, "most of us live our lives trying to win approval from the people in the outer circles. It's all part of the conspiracy. It's as if the Fallen One snuck in while we were sleeping and rearranged our values. Suddenly the things that matter the most were cheapened and made to appear less desirable. At the same time, the things that are temporary, things that have no eternal value, were made to appear priceless, and attractive, and of ultimate importance. So this is what I have for you. Write this down, and when you have doubts, when you have a question about what matters or a decision that will involve your family and your future, draw the circles. *Live to impress the inner circles.* If you have to choose between making your kids happy or making the people at work happy, choose the kids.

We need to learn how to live in such a way that we impress the inner circles.

If it comes down to disappointing your friends or your family, disappoint your friends. And now hear me on this," she said. "If you're forced to please your wife or your mother, please your wife. Always press in toward the inner circles. Always!"

I walked her out to the car and said, "Mom, I don't want you to go. There's so much more I want to say, so much more I want to do, and so much more I want to ask you. What is this conspiracy that everybody is talking about, and what did you mean when you said the Fallen One snuck in while we were sleeping? Everyone is talking in riddles. What does it mean and what does any of it have to do with me?"

"I can't tell you everything," Mom answered. "You have to feel your way along on this a little bit at a time. But I can tell you this. The Fallen One is the ancient adversary, the serpent who seduced Adam and Eve in the Garden. The morning star cast out of heaven. He goes by many names—some call him Satan, others call him the devil, still others call him Beelzebub or Lucifer or the Prince of Darkness. But whatever you call him, he is the tempter and the accuser of humanity. Like a shooting star he was flung from heaven, and since that day the angels refuse to even whisper his name. Any evil comes from him. He's behind it all, even the accident.

"Look at me," she continued, putting my face in her hands and turning my head toward hers. "That's on him, not you, do you hear me? Somewhere you got the idea that it was your fault. It wasn't. Sometimes bad things happen. You need to believe that, Sky."

It was a moment between a mother and a son that needed to take place. Lord knows, I wanted to believe her, I needed to believe her, but somehow I just couldn't. Things you've held onto for so long are hard to let go of, even if they're wrong.

She could tell I was struggling, and so she continued. "Nothing happened that can't be rewoven back into the fabric of God's plan. He's still in charge of Ben's life, and yours. Sometimes things happen that we all wish hadn't happened. Sometimes it looks like evil has gotten the upper hand. But that's just a momentary interruption in the flow of things. God's plan is like a river—it winds, it turns, it might even get dammed up once in a while, but in the end, its force is unstoppable."

"I know that's true," I said. "But sometimes it doesn't feel like it. Jesus may have conquered sin and death on the first Easter, but I see the power of evil every day in my line of work. Divorce, addiction, abuse, guilt, failure—these things can bring even the strongest to their knees. I'm sorry, Mom, but some days it seems like Satan is winning."

"Listen," Mom countered. "I know that sometimes life isn't fair. It feels like Satan and Ahbee are equals in the battle of good and evil, but nothing is further from the truth. Satan is no match for him. Satan is Michael's counterpart. Once the two of them were alike in every way. In the time before time began their strength, beauty, and magnificence were unequaled among the ranks of the angels. But then Satan was tripped up by his own desires, and ever since that day he's tried his best to pull the rest of the world down with him.

"I would love to tell you more, but I can't. I've stayed too long already. Besides, that's what eternity is all about. This was just supposed to be a little taste of that. But if you're still hungry, I left you a little something in the fridge."

As she was getting into the car I said, "I love you, Mom."

"I love you too," she replied. Then she kissed me good-bye, closed the car door, and drove away.

Back inside I looked in the fridge, and there was a pie covered in meringue with a note that said, "Grandma Jacobs sends her love."

Every Thanksgiving, my mother would make the meal I had just eaten, and Grandma would make a butterscotch pie like the one I found in the fridge.

I cut myself a big slice of memories, poured a glass of milk, and went upstairs to bed.

self-examination

Nothing will make us so charitable and tender
to the faults of others, as, by self-examination,
thoroughly to know our own.

François Fénelon

7

You're on your own today, Scout," Ahbee said as I came downstairs for breakfast. "It's a beautiful day outside, and I think you need to take a walk down by the creek and do a little thinking. You've had a lot of stuff thrown your way, and maybe you should try to unpack some of it on your own."

I noticed the creek the day I arrived. The lake narrowed just past the mailbox, and then it spilled over a little dam and flowed under an old iron bridge. It called out to be explored, and this was as good a time as any. And now I knew why there were water shoes at the end of the bed where I'd left my sandals the night before.

Nothing happens by accident here, I thought to myself.

"Or anywhere else," Ahbee said as he laid two blueberry pancakes on the plate in front of me. "There is always a plan, even when you can't see it."

"I wanted to talk to you about that," I said. "I never understood how Ben's accident could be part of your plan."

"Just put your dishes in the sink when you're done," he said, walking toward the kitchen. "And as for the accident, we'll talk more about that later."

When I opened my eyes after saying the blessing, Ahbee was

gone. He'd left an old Cub Scout knapsack lying on the kitchen table. Beside it was a note addressed to me that said, "Enjoy the walk and the lunch," and I knew I was on my own.

God always has a plan, even when we can't see it.

After breakfast, I walked down the road toward the west end of the lake where it spilled into the creek, and that's when I noticed the U-shaped swimming dock. It looked exactly like the one by the public beach all those years ago. Suddenly my mind was full of memories I'd kept hidden in a dark corner of my soul for twenty-five years.

It was the Fourth of July weekend. I'd taken a MasterCraft boat in on trade the week before, and to be honest I kind of buried us in by putting a little more money into it than it was worth, but I'd promised Ben that I'd take him and his friends up north skiing for the weekend, and a promise is a promise.

Mom and Dad had rented this big cottage for the month of July, and we were all going up there for a long weekend. We needed a break. I'd been working sixty-five-hour weeks at the dealership, and Ben was in football camp at State. Michigan, Iowa, Nebraska, and Florida had recruited him pretty hard in high school, but there was never any doubt where he was going. Ben had been a State fan since he was a little kid, and for him, college was all about football.

Like Dad, he'd lettered in both baseball and basketball three years running, but as a freshman, he was the starting quarterback from day one. Dad had named him Benjamin, which means "son of my right hand," and he was. Like Dad, he was a natural athlete. It came easy to him. I was Schuyler, the scholar, the other son, the left-handed one. I played a little ball too, but never like Ben. He was just special. And he was so likeable that even though I was a little jealous of him, I still couldn't help but admire him, and so, like Dad, I never missed one of his games.

With Ben as quarterback, the Indians won the city champion-ship in his sophomore year and district in his junior year, and they finished second in the state when he was a senior. They should have won it, but Johnson dropped two passes in the end zone, and then Wallace fumbled on the seven with a minute forty to go. Everybody knew the Indians were contenders because of Ben. He was big, strong, fast, and accurate, and college coaches got weak in the knees when they watched him on film. When Bucky recruited him, he said, "Give me two years, three at the top, and you'll go pro." And we all believed him.

The incoming freshman class was full of superstars. Mickey Davis was coming from Catholic Day at right guard, and nobody got past him. At six foot four and two-eighty, he was built like a refrigerator. They said that Mickey didn't have calves, he had cows, and seeing him in swim trunks made me think they were right. Ben could almost be assured that he'd never get blindsided with Mickey in there.

Rafer "the Rabbit" Washington from downstate had already signed as wide receiver. He was lightning quick, with hands like fly traps, and he could jump like a rabbit—hence the name. Rafer was tall and lean with olive skin and a boyish grin. He didn't say much, but his game said it all.

And then the coup de grace was that Billy "White-Shoes" Barber, the sophomore tailback who'd set every running record State had, was back for at least one more year. Now with Ben inked to a full-ride scholarship, Bucky was starting training camp with the best weapons he'd ever had, and he'd coached some great ones.

Bucky had been pushing them hard, maybe too hard if you asked me, with two-a-day practices, mandatory film meetings every night, and regular workouts in the weight room. Bucky wanted Ben to put on twenty pounds. He said at six foot four and two-fifty-five, he'd be unstoppable. And he was right about that. The problem was, the pressure was starting to layer up, and a little R & R was just what they needed. That's why I buried myself in that boat.

Bucky had gotten them a State van, and they were all sitting on the beach around a cooler of drinks when I got there. They were talking sports with Dad, and Ben told them about how Dad had tried out with the White Sox, but when he told them that he'd promised his mother he wouldn't play on Sundays, they sent him packing without so much as a train ticket home. Billy White-Shoes was howling with laughter, and his gold front tooth sparkled in the sunlight.

"I've never heard anything so crazy," he said. "Jesus don't care if you play baseball on Sunday. If you get a chance like that, he expects you to take it. That's what talent is all about. It gets you a shot, and then it's use it or lose it." Billy was a kid from the streets of Chicago who grew up fighting. After football season, his senior year of high school, he got in a little trouble running with the Black P-Stone Nation. When he got arrested, his momma got Bucky to talk some of the athletic boosters into quietly putting up his bail and getting him an expensive attorney. When the charges were dropped, Bucky told him he'd better clean up his act or he could forget all about his football scholarship. He did.

"My momma sent me down here with only one request," Billy said. "She told me I better make the best of this 'cause God don't go handing out a lot of chances in our neighborhood, and I intend to do just that. I came real close to declaring myself eligible for the draft, but when Bucky told me that Ben was inked, I decided to play one more year. If we can win a bowl game, there's no limit to what my signing bonus might be, and then I'm going to buy my momma a brick house."

Micky and Rafer agreed. Each of them was a great athlete, but football is a team sport, and when the team wins, they all win. And like every kid who ever put on a helmet, they all dreamed of going to the pros. But that day was about relaxing. They wanted to eat some steaks, get some sun, and check out the girls on the beach.

"Hey bro," Ben said. "Why don't you put that MasterCraft in the lake, and I'll show these boys how to water-ski."

"You sure you'll be all right?" I said. "Looks like you've had a few brewskis."

"Don't you worry about me," he said. "But I'm not sure these landlubbers can handle it." He bantered back and forth with his teammates while I put the boat in the water. I pulled up to the dock and asked Rafer if he wanted to ride along and spot for me.

"Sure," he said. "But I don't know what spotting is." I told him that the spotter sits in the back of the boat and tells the driver if something happens. Rafer had never been water-skiing, so watching someone else do it sounded like a good idea to him. I told him to sit down in the rear-facing observation seat and hold on.

While we were talking Ben grabbed the slalom ski and a life jacket, turned to Billy, and said, "This is how you do it without getting your afro wet."

"Don't worry about me," Billy said. "I've done this a few times before. Just don't embarrass yourself too bad in front of the cheerleaders."

The boat was a serious ski boat, with a direct drive 220 horsepower inboard that rumbled and snorted at idle like a racehorse in the starting gate. This baby wanted to run. It had a white hull with a wide blue strip that said MASTERCRAFT in cut-out white letters on the side, and there was a vertical American flag in the stripe near the transom. At idle and at speed it laid low in the water, and even with a skier the boat was extraordinarily stable.

When we pulled up by the U-shaped swimming dock, a group of girls walked over from the public beach to watch, and I knew Ben was going to give them a show. I threw him the ski rope and started to pull the boat away from the beach. Ben slipped the ski on his left foot, lifted it off the dock, dangled it over the water, and stood there balancing on his right. Then, with three coils of the rope still floating on the water, he yelled, "Hit it!"

I threw the throttle forward and the boat lunged into motion. Just as the ski rope became taut, Ben stepped onto the ski, creating a huge spray of water, and we were off. He'd been skiing since he was seven, and he was an expert. We pulled over to the other side of the lake where someone had set up a slalom course and took a pass at it. Ben pulled hard on the rope with his right arm, leaned on his back foot, and with water spraying eight feet in the air, he cut across the right wake. With his shoulder inches off the water, he easily went around the first buoy. He stood up straight, waved to the girls on the beach, and then pulled hard with his left arm, leaned in the opposite direction, and went screaming back across both wakes to circle the second buoy.

Right, left, right, left, stretching and pulling and leaning, he methodically worked his way through the course. After he hit every one, we circled back around by the beach to drop him off. When we got there again he pulled hard on his right arm and went racing toward the shore, but right before he went smashing into the beach, he leaned back, twisted the ski in a spiral, sent water flying in every direction, and stepped out of the ski in ankle-deep water.

"Your turn, Billy," he said, and he handed him the ski and the vest. Surprisingly, Billy was a great skier. His first pass through the slalom course he missed two buoys, but by the end of the day he'd gotten every one. Mickey knew how to ski, but barely. He hung on for dear life on two skis, and when he tried to drop one he lost his balance and went bouncing across the water like a skipping stone.

It was an afternoon of too much sun, too much beer, and too much laughing, and it was exactly what they needed to unwind. All three of them had been teasing Rafer unmercifully about not skiing, and finally, about five thirty, he agreed to try it. Mickey and Billy helped him get the skis on. "Hit it," yelled Mickey, and Rafer popped out of the water like a bobber on a cane pole. He wobbled like a Weeble for about 150 yards and then went plunging into the water.

I pulled back around and circled in close to him. "Ya okay?" I asked.

"I think so," he said, but I could tell that he'd swallowed a lot of water.

While he struggled to get his skis on, I put the boat in neutral, and Ben went back onto the swim platform to see if he could help with the rope. The current was pushing us back toward Rafer, and Ben was worried the tow rope would get fouled in the prop. He reached around the back with his right hand and grabbed the rope near the tow hook on the transom. Then, facing forward and still holding on, he leaned back trying to take up the slack with his left hand and keep it from fouling, but it wasn't enough.

"Put her in gear and ease forward a little," he said, still leaning back and trying to whip the rope away from the prop as he balanced precariously on the back of the swim platform.

"Be careful," I said. "That teak wood can get slippery when it's wet." But with the girls watching the show from the beach, he ignored me.

"Take up the slack now," he said, "or we'll be cutting that rope off the prop with a jackknife."

When I pushed the throttle forward, I didn't realize that the steering wheel was cocked to the left, and for a split second the boat lunged ahead in that direction. It caught Ben by surprise, and he almost did a header off the right side of the swim platform. Unfortunately, he tried to catch himself by jerking on the rope with his right hand, and as I straightened out the boat, instinctively he kicked out his left foot for balance. He briefly balanced there acrobatically and then plunged into the water. When he did, his left foot was clipped by the propeller blade.

Even all these years later, the next few minutes are kind of a blur in my mind. As I circled around again with the boat, Ben's head bobbed up out of the water, and he screamed in agony. I thought he was horsing around until I saw the blood. It looked like a scene from *Jaws*. There was blood in the water everywhere, and when I managed to get him in the boat I wrapped his foot in a beach towel and raced for shore.

The county Sheriff had been taking a coffee break on a picnic table under the oak trees in the grass above the beach, and when he heard Ben scream he came a-running. With lights flashing and the siren screaming, he took Dad and me and Ben to Mercy Hospital. The only thing I remember from the sixteen-mile drive was Dad. He was calm—too calm. He had wrapped his shirt around Ben's foot like a tourniquet and then wrapped his arms around Ben.

"It'll be all right," he said. Over and over again he said it—"It'll be all right"—but we all knew it wouldn't be all right.

They rushed Ben into surgery, and about four hours later the doctor came out to see us. His name was Alan Swartz; he was a thin, good-looking man with silver hair and a pencil-thin mustache. We later learned that he was a pioneer in what's called silicone small joint implants, an incredibly complex procedure that involved bone shaping and rebalancing of the surrounding joint tissue. Swartz developed the surgery for people suffering from severe arthritis. But by sheer luck and God's grace he was there for a conference the day Ben needed him.

"He's lucky," Dr. Swartz said. "It could have been a lot worse. It looks like the propeller blade only struck him once, and it was a clean cut. It severed the proximal of the hallux and the metatarsals of the next two phalanx."

"Can you put that in English?" Dad said, and Swartz obliged.

"The blade of the propeller cut through the major joint of the big toe and the lower bones of the next two. It also severed the cords and tendons. Some of the bone is missing, and there was some debris that needed to be cleaned out, but after that we were able to put an implant in and pin things back together. In time he should heal pretty well."

"What do you mean, pretty well?" Dad asked. "Will he walk, will he run?"

"Sure, he'll walk. He might have a slight limp, but he'll walk fine. He won't be much of a runner, at least not for a while, but maybe someday. It'll be months before he can put any real weight on it, and it won't be as flexible as it once was, but he'll walk. He's lucky," Swartz said. "His toes were hanging on by a thread. A couple millimeters more and they'd have been fish food." He could see Dad wince and he apologized. "Sorry. I just mean if he'd have lost his toes in the lake, he'd walk pretty gimpy for the rest of his life. But now, like I said, I think in six months to a year he'll be walking around fine, and after that, who knows? A lot of it'll be up to him."

Dad and I both knew what that meant. No football. That was the foot he needed to plant if he was going to pass with any accuracy. Nobody can throw off their back foot very well, at least not with any consistency.

My sister, Sharon, kept calling the hospital, and finally, after a couple of hours, she and Mom showed up at the hospital with Billy, Rafer, and Mickey. When they walked in I realized that I'd left Rafer sitting out in the lake when I brought Ben back to shore.

"Sorry, man," I said. "I didn't mean to leave you out there, but . . ."

"You don't need to explain," he said. "How's your brother? Is he going to be okay?"

"They stitched him up," I said. "He was lucky, there was some hotshot specialist that happened to be here, and now we'll have to wait and see."

"But he'll be able to play, right?" Billy looked at me inquisitively. "He'll still be able to play ball?"

That's when Dad broke down. He put his face in his hands

and started crying uncontrollably. Mom sat down beside him and said, "It'll be all right, honey, don't worry."

"No, it won't," he said. "Everybody keeps saying that, but it won't be all right." Then he looked at me and said, "What do you think you were doing out there, Sky? How could you let this happen? I told you to keep an eye on him!"

For a minute, his words froze everything in the room. No one moved or said a word, but Dad's words cut me like a knife. He didn't say anything I wasn't thinking, but hearing it, especially from him, made it real. I'd been trying to hide from it, but there was no hiding anymore. The weight of it crushed in on me, and I crumpled in the chair.

"That's not fair," Sharon said. "It's not Sky's fault. It was an accident—a terrible, horrible accident."

"Accident or not," Dad said, "all of this never would have happened if Sky hadn't brought that boat up here to show off. I told him, 'no horsing around, these boys are in training, what they need is rest.' I promised Bucky that I'd keep an eye on them, and then Sky showed up."

"He was just trying to show them a good time, help them unwind a little," Sharon said.

"Look," Dad said. "These boys are special, irreplaceable on the football field. You got to be careful with people like that. You don't let them put themselves in harm's way."

"Ben's a big boy; he can look out for himself!"

"Obviously he can't," Dad said. "Great athletes are like racehorses. They need constant care. If you've got a plow mule, you work it hard all day and then you just let it graze for its supper in the field at night. But if you've got a racehorse, that's a whole different ball game. You give them the best oats, the best hay, the best of everything. You hire the best groomers, and trainers, and vets, and jockeys because racehorses are special. You take every precaution you can because you've got a lot invested in them, and, well, all I was saying is that a lot of us have got a lot invested in Ben."

"He's not a racehorse, Dad; he's your son. So is Sky, and blaming him for this isn't going to fix anything. You're the one who wanted these boys to break training and come up here for a few days. And if you remember, I'm the one who suggested that we go water-skiing."

"You're right," Dad said, looking up at Sharon. "I don't know what I was thinking. I'm sorry, Sky. Forgive me," he said, reaching over and putting his hand on my knee. "It was an accident, just a freak accident. No one's to blame."

But hearing him say it didn't change anything. You can't take words like that back. I felt guilty before he said it, and hearing it from my father only confirmed my guilt.

"I'm sorry, Dad," I said. "I don't know what else I can say. I'm sorry."

He put his hand up as if to say, "That's enough!" and then he slowly shook his head, looked at the floor, and let out a long, deep sigh. The grief of it all washed over him, and he and my mother fell into each other's arms. I knew our conversation was over, and I also knew that my guilt wasn't over. Whatever my culpability was, it was something I was going to have to learn to live with.

Of course, logically I also knew that some of this was on Ben. He was always pressing the limits. It was his nature. Some kids are natural-born risk takers. As little kids we were given boundaries. Don't touch that; it's hot. Don't go out of the yard; it's not safe. Don't color outside the lines. Then as we got a little older, we learned that every game we played had lines that defined what was in bounds and what was out. But some kids just don't think the rules apply to them. That was Ben. He was always pressing the limits, and so Dad was right: knowing that, I should have been watching out for him.

Since then I've replayed that day a million times in my head, but I still don't know what I'd do different. All I know is that I wish I'd done something different.

The boys went in and saw Ben and made some remarks about him maybe missing a game or two.

"We'll let Bucky know what happened," Billy said. "Keep us posted, okay?"

"We will," Dad said.

"I'll pray," Rafer said.

The other two said, "We'll pray too," and they meant it. Then they got in the van and went back to the university.

For the next few months we all prayed. On the eve of State's first game there was a pep rally, and afterwards they filled the field house for a prayer meeting for Ben. He was there with crutches, and when he dropped them and gingerly walked across the stage, the place erupted in applause. For the whole summer and most of the fall we all believed in miracles. We hoped, we dreamed, and we prayed that Ben would be able to play again next season, but God didn't answer that prayer. Winter term Ben dropped out of school, and he never went back.

When I think about the accident now, one of two things happens. I either get angry or I feel guilty, and today it was a little of both. I was angry with Ahbee for picking the scab off an old wound. If he knew everything, then he knew that I've always carried a piece of the guilt from that day around with me wherever I went. Sometimes it would get buried under the busyness of the day, and other times it would come bubbling up to the surface. Sometimes when it did, the only thing that would get me through it was the memory of hearing my dad say it was an accident. Now even that small comfort was taken from me when Ahbee said, "Nothing happens by accident here, or anywhere else." If that's true, then someone's to blame for everything, and so the accident was either on me or it was on Ahbee.

For a while I sat on the beach and wrestled with my guilt. Then I cried for what felt like an hour or more. Finally, when my storehouse of tears ran dry, I got angry.

"Is this what you wanted me to unpack, Ahbee?" I shouted. "Do you enjoy watching people reopen old wounds? Is that your game? Are you trying to push my nose in it? Well, two can play at that game, you know. If you are who you say you are, if you're all-powerful and all-knowing, then you either should have seen the accident coming or you should have stopped it. Either way, some of this is on you. You could have done something and chose not to. So tell me, if you can, what kind of a loving Father would stand by and watch his children suffer? If Rae is right, if you're always with me, then answer me. Show yourself, you coward. This has been brewing between us for a long time. Let's have it out once and for all."

I knew that like in my younger years, I was picking a fight I couldn't win, but I didn't care. I wanted an answer. "Explain yourself!" I shouted, sounding more like Job than I intended.

For the longest time I waited for a response—a voice, or a lightning bolt, or something—but it never came. As he so often does, God held his tongue, and the callous silence became my answer. I was exhausted and at the same time exhilarated. I'd been waiting a long time to get that off my chest. Finally I decided to walk off a little of my anger by wading in the creek.

It was cold and clear, and as I stepped in, sand billowed up from the bottom. Minnows darted in every direction at once, and a nervous box turtle flopped off a log to my left and disappeared into the willows. I walked slowly and tried to take in the nature around me. Birds chirped in the breeze, and as I made my way with the slow-moving current, I'd see a bluegill or a perch or a school of minnows slip silently past my legs every once in a while.

In places the creek was lined with birch trees and tall, wispy white pines that spilled into a dense and dark woods. Then around the next bend, rock cliffs rose up from the water, and the bottom of the creek would turn from sand to smooth, round stones. I saw a blue heron leapfrogging his way in flight in front of me, and a couple of mallards skidded in for a landing on the water over my shoulder.

Ahbee was right: it was peaceful. The cool water quenched the fire in my soul. The more I walked, the better I felt. Each step seemed to lighten my load. Maybe it was time. I'd been carrying this around bottled up inside me for too long.

"I'm sorry, God," I whispered. "Sometimes it's easier to just lay all this at your door and walk away. I know that's not fair. There's more than enough blame to go around. But like my mom said, sometimes the world isn't fair, and, well, I'm part of that world." Once again I waited for a response, but the only thing I heard was the wind rustling through the trees. "Is that you, Rae?" I asked hopefully. But if it was, she, like Ahbee, kept silent, so I kept wading my way along.

The more I thought about it the more I realized that this was the perfect place to unpack my thoughts. There were a few cottages along the way, mostly on top of the rock cliffs. Once in a while I could hear voices, but for the most part I was alone with my thoughts and my prayers. Someone once said that when we're having trouble putting the pieces of life into perspective, we should pray. And they were right: we don't pray enough. Prayer changes everything, but worry changes nothing, so I decided to try and pray more and worry less.

Prayer changes everything, but worry changes nothing.

I walked and prayed my way down the creek, and when the water turned dark, I'd skirt the edges to keep from getting too wet. In some places it looked like the water was over my head, but mostly it was up to my knees with rocks and rapids.

By late morning I'd walked the full length of the creek and found myself on the shores of a huge body of fresh water that was rimmed with sand dunes and squawking seagulls. Whitecaps crashed against the shore, and a wind blew in off the lake. It seemed like a good place to eat my lunch, so I sat down on a piece of driftwood and unloaded the knapsack that had been left for me on the kitchen table.

Inside the knapsack was a Granny Smith apple, a half-melted Milky Way, a bag of Fritos, some celery sticks with peanut butter, a brown sugar and oleo sandwich on Wonder bread, and a chocolate cherry macaroon.

How can this be? I thought to myself. *These macaroons are my own secret recipe. And someone's been talking to my mother. This is exactly the kind of lunch she would have made when I was a kid.*

The macaroon recipe was originally my mother's, but over the years I doubled their size, added the dried cherries, and dipped them in dark chocolate. I guess Ahbee approved of my additions.

As I ate my lunch, I looked out at the lake, listened to the seagulls, and thought about the people I had been talking to over the past few days. Moments slipped into hours. If I was dreaming, I didn't want to wake up. Then it hit me—this must be what heaven is like!

Lightning cracked on the big lake's horizon, and it was as if Ahbee were calling me back to the cottage. Huge black clouds rolled in toward the dunes. Then it began raining—first one raindrop, then another, and by the time I made my way back to the cottage, I was drenched and shivering. I was hoping to see a familiar car in the driveway, but there was none to be found. *I guess it's a day off from everything*, I thought to myself.

Inside the kitchen, I took off my wet water shoes and called out, but no one answered. I went upstairs and took a warm shower, and when I was finished, my clothes were laid out on the bed as always: a hooded Hope College sweatshirt, blue jeans, rag socks, and sandals.

I made myself a sandwich from last night's leftovers and went out on the screened-in porch. The sun had broken through and was slowly setting over the treetops on the west end of the lake. I sat watching the lights turn on in the houses across the lake.

Someone had started a bonfire, and I could just make out the silhouettes of three little girls lighting sparklers and roasting marshmallows. It had been a long time since Kate, Kelly, and Tara were that age, but seeing these girls made me miss my own. They were grown women now, and if you asked me, they grew up far too quickly.

I remembered how they'd come running at me with their arms open when I'd walk through the back door after a long day. "We missed you, Daddy," they'd say. "Why aren't you home more?"

I always had a good excuse. "I had people who needed me," I'd say. "And your daddy tries to make them better." At least that's what I'd tell myself. I had to go by the hospital, I had to teach a class, I had to meet with someone else's mommy and daddy who didn't love each other like their mommy and I. My list of excuses was impressive. The world needed a superman, and I had a red cape. But looking back at it all now, I'm not so sure God would have minded that much if I'd spent a little less time with other people's families and a little more time with my own.

Everyone loves to be included in a story.

Even so, I'm a lucky man. I have great kids—mostly, I suppose, because they had a great mother, but still, I want to believe that I had a little something to do with it. For example, each night before they went to sleep, I'd say their prayers with them, tell them a story, and try my best to listen as they told me about their day.

Sometimes we'd read a story, but most of the time we made up our own. I'd always begin by saying, "Once upon a time, not your time, or my time, but a time lost in time itself, there lived three beautiful princesses named Katrina, Kelcinda, and Taratanna." After that I'd invite them to help me imagine the story. I'd say, "They were on their way to . . . ," and then I'd stop and ask them where they thought the princesses were going.

Children have wonderful imaginations, so immediately one of them would pipe up and say they were going to the fair, or shopping, or to their grandma's house, or to a baseball game. And I'd say, "That's right!" and weave their idea into the story.

"It was a beautiful spring day, and they were on their way to the fair. It came to town once a year, and it was always wonderful. Beautifully painted horse-drawn wagons would roll down Main Street and set up their tents and booths in the vacant field down by the river. The girls had watched the wagons ride by their castle yesterday afternoon, and so all night their dreams were filled with elephants, monkeys, Ferris wheels, and big sticky pieces of pink cotton candy. The next morning they were thinking about what they were going to do at the fair, when suddenly . . ." And again I'd ask them to imagine the story with me.

"Suddenly they came to a river," Kate would say. Kate loves rivers. Or, "Suddenly there was a handsome prince riding a beautiful polka-dotted horse." Or, "Suddenly there was a giant sitting in the middle of the road."

"Yes," I'd say. "That's exactly what happened. There was a huge one-eyed giant sitting in the middle of the road. He was barefoot with nothing on but a faded old pair of farmer jeans, and he was a sight to see. He had light green skin, orange hair, and a big red eye that was crying pink tears. Well, the girls weren't sure if they should offer to help him or run away, but then Taratanna walked up, gave him her handkerchief, and asked, 'Why are you crying?' And he replied . . . What did he say, Kelly?"

We could stop the story almost anywhere and pick it up again the next night because it really wasn't a lot of different stories as much as it was one big never-ending story. Of course, there came a time when the girls outgrew stories, and in a way they outgrew me too.

So years later, one of my best days was right before Tara got married. All three girls were home, which was a rarity, and we were up at Dad's cottage. I went in to say good-night, and they said, "Dad, would you tell us a story?" So I unpacked the three beautiful princesses from the attic of my memory, and Katrina,

Kelcinda, and Taratanna went on one more adventure. When they were young, the stories were my gift to them, but on that night, story time was their gift to me. It warmed my heart to know that those bedtime stories meant as much to them as they had to me.

"Once upon a time," I said. "Not your time, or my time, but a time lost in time itself . . ." And as I remembered our stories, I realized that Rae was right. We really do learn not by memorizing creeds and confessions but by the stories of our lives. Jesus never once wrote down a list of rules for us to live by, but the Gospels are full of his stories.

In a file in my office I kept three letters that I'd written to my children, a separate one for each girl. I started writing them years ago after I got a call from a friend of mine named Matt. He told me they'd just found out that his wife, Kathy, had cancer, and he wondered if they could come by and talk about it.

"Of course," I said, and a couple hours later they were sitting in my office. She had inoperable brain cancer, and it was only a matter of months. We talked through it, we cried, and we prayed, and I tried to be as clinical as I could. They were friends, and they needed me to help them make a list of things they had to do before she died. I said they should make an appointment with their pastor, and their lawyer, and their insurance man, and they also really needed to get a second opinion to make sure.

"We know all that," Matt said. "What we need to know from you is, how do we explain this to our boys?"

They had two sons: Kevin, who was eight, and Kyle, who was five. I encouraged them to be honest but also age appropriate.

"Answer their questions," I said. "Tell them you love them, and read them this." I gave them a copy of a children's book I had about heaven. We paged through it together, and Matt asked if I believed in heaven. I said that I did, and he slowly nodded his head as if to say, "Yeah, me too." After a few minutes they thanked me for my time and stood up to leave.

I walked them to the door and then, right as they were leaving, I suggested to Kathy that she might want to write the boys some letters.

"They could open them on special days," I said. "Like their next birthday, or the day they graduate from high school, or the day they get married, or maybe when they make profession of faith." I'm not sure where the idea came from, but she liked it.

"In some ways then it would be like I was there," she said, and I agreed. The thought of writing the letters seemed to bring her some comfort, and she asked me if I would be willing to help her write them.

"Sure, we can do that," I said, and so each Monday for the next two months we met and wrote what she called her "I love you letters." Each one seemed more poignant and more honest than the last. To be honest, the letters tore at my soul. I couldn't stop thinking about them, and that's when I decided to write some letters of my own.

Every year on Father's Day, after everyone else was asleep, I'd stay up and read them. Periodically through the years I'd rewrite them, and when I did I'd burn the old ones. I'd sit alone in the dark in front of the fireplace and say, "My Father which art in heaven, help me be a better father here on earth."

Then sometimes I'd go in the girls' bedrooms and wake them up to tell them how much I loved them and how proud I was to be their dad. I'd promise them that this year was going to be different, that I'd play more Monopoly and make more popcorn and take more time off from work, and I meant it.

As a dad I'm a work in progress, and I think I'm getting better at it. The problem is that with each new letter I write, they have less need of me.

I'm not sure when it happened, or how, or why, but somehow in the mystery of God's timing they all tiptoed into womanhood when I wasn't looking. They are competent and confident. They don't need me to teach them how to play T-ball, or ride a bike, or untangle their fishing line, and it's hard on my ego. I want to be needed. It's part of who I am. For much of my adult life I've been Kate, Kelly, and Tara's dad, and I've so enjoyed it. I was their coach, and their counselor, and their biggest cheerleader in life.

Even in their teen years when it seemed like their moods changed about as often as they changed their clothes—even then, and maybe especially then, I prayed for them, and loved them, and tried to hold back the reins as they ran unbridled into adulthood. But I couldn't stop them. They grew up anyway.

To be honest, if I could, I'd rewind the clock to the days when they'd greet me at the back door giggling and shouting, "Daddy's home!" I miss bouncing them on my knee, and tickling their chubby little toes, and telling bedtime stories, and listening to their bedtime prayers, and solving their little problems. I liked it when all their problems were little. But now I'm afraid the creeping giant of change has had its way with us all. They're all grown up now, and I've grown old. Not ancient, not decrepit, but old enough to know what my dad meant when he'd say, "I can't believe where the time has gone."

There's a little voice in my head that wants to scream, *Stop! Don't go! There's so much more I want to teach you.* But then there's another voice, a wiser voice, their mother's voice! She reminds me that they've learned their lessons long ago, and they'll be fine without me now.

There are certain words that are washed in the emotion of a particular moment in time and never meant for publication. The "I love you letters" were those kind of words. But whenever words like that are published, the reader needs to enter into a kind of sacred trust with the writer.

It's like when Jesus was baptized and he heard God say, "This is my beloved Son, with whom I am well pleased." I imagine that at that very moment, if we would have been there, we'd have heard the whispered words of God in the rustling wind.

"Shhh . . . ," he said. "Hush now, let all the earth keep silent, for

I have something special to say to my Son." And what followed was what every child wants to hear, for there are no sweeter words in a child's ear than the praise of a parent.

The "I love you letters" were those kinds of words, and now that the girls have grown I no longer feel a need to continually rewrite them each year. Many of the big milestone moments in their lives have come and gone, and I've been able to share my heart with each of them in person. Not surprisingly, in each case some of the words from their letters have spilled from my lips.

For example, when Kelly went off to college, I stood in the shadow of Gilmore Hall and told her that her excitement brought me great joy.

"I know you want this," I said. "And I know you're ready to be on your own, but forgive me if I'm not quite ready to let you go. The world has a lot of rough edges, and I wanted to protect you from all that just a little longer. But like a baby bird perched on the edge of her nest, you are ready to test your wings, and I must let you go. But that doesn't stop me from worrying. You see, I know you, and I know how willing you are to make other people's problems your own. You have a tender heart and a listening ear, and if you're not careful people will take advantage of that, and, well, even the strongest among us have a load limit."

As I assembled the loft in her dorm room, Kelly went back home for another load of stuff, and my mind went back to an incident earlier that year. I so wanted to say, "Kelly, remember last year when Casey's mom, Laura, took her own life? She was a good woman—kind, sympathetic, and always ready to open her door or her heart to anyone who was hurting. The caseload of her practice read like a laundry list of battered women and abused children. They would come and lie on her couch and unpack the suitcases of their lives one problem at a time. When they left, they always felt lighter, as if a load had been lifted off their shoulders, but she always felt heavier. Worry is like a cancer that eats up the joy in your soul, and that's what happened to Laura. She strapped their problems on her back like a knapsack, and eventually the weight of it took its toll.

"After they left she would pick up the tearstained Kleenex scattered around her couch and throw them away, but it was as if their tears stuck to her like glue. She began to cry for no reason, and when her husband, Jack, would ask her what was the matter, she would say, 'Nothing, it's nothing.' But it was something, and the more that something grew, the more the distance grew between the two of them. When Jack would ask her to go out for dinner or to a movie or to the Friday night football game over at the high school, she'd say, 'I'd love to but I have some reading to do,' or some paperwork, or a client in crisis, and she'd send him off alone. And that's when she started drinking.

"Jack came to me once, a few months before she died, and he said, 'I don't know what to do, Sky. I feel like dark forces have broken into my house in the dark of night and stolen my wife. She never laughs anymore, never wants to do anything with me and the kids, and never wants me to hold her. You've got to help me, Sky. Maybe she'll listen to you.' I tried, but she was in denial. 'I've just got a particularly heavy caseload right now,' she said. 'It'll lighten up this summer.' By summer she was gone."

My train of thought was interrupted as Kelly came back into the room carrying an armload of clothes.

"Hi, Dad," she said. "Looks like you've about got the loft together."

"This is the last bolt," I said, "but before I go, come over here, give me a hug, and let me finish what I was saying earlier."

She hung up the clothes, put her arm around my neck, and said, "Don't make me cry, Dad."

I spoke slowly and deliberately. "Guard your heart, Kelly. Be careful who you let in. I want you to have lots of friends, and to fall in love, and to care about the broken people of the world, but I don't want them to break your heart. Like your mother, you have a generous spirit. You're always ready to give of yourself to anyone who asks, and I love that about you, but be careful, okay? And when life starts piling up and you need to unload a little, call me. I'll always be there. Okay?"

"Sure, Dad," she said. "But you didn't need to say it. I always knew you were there for me."

My conversation with Kate came the second summer she went out to Colorado to work at Noah's Ark. It was the premier white-water rafting company on the Arkansas River, and for Kate it quickly became a second home. I knew that she loved the mountains, the white-water rafting, and the adventure, and the people there were some of her closest friends. Like her they were all young and passionate, and they lived with an intensity for life and for God. I also knew that she went intending to again only spend the summer out there, but there was a part of me that was afraid that this time she'd never come back home.

She left for Colorado early in the morning on a beautiful spring day as the sun was just peeking over the eastern skyline. Her silver Subaru Baja was packed and parked in the driveway, ready for the long cross-country trip. We'd had breakfast, and her mother and her sisters had already said their tearful good-byes. Now the two of us sat alone together in the front seat of her truck.

"You have your cell phone?" I asked, knowing she did.

"Yes, Dad," she replied.

"And the GPS?"

"It's right there on the dash, and you helped me plug in the coordinates last night. Besides, I've made this trip before, you know. Just like last year, I've got reservations at the Best Western in Kearney, Nebraska, and I'll call you when I get there. Don't worry, Dad, I'll be fine!"

"I know you will," I said. "You've got that same stubborn, independent streak that your Grandma Jackie's famous for." My kids always called Jackie the fun grandma, mostly because she never really grew up and so she'd let them get away with almost anything. She always had candy, costumes, and the latest toys and games, and she was always ready to play. Baseball, Slip 'N Slide, Super Soaker squirt guns, fireworks, ice skates, lawn darts, and hula hoops—if it was fun, Jackie had it. Like I said, she was always a kid at heart.

During World War II, when all the able-bodied men went off to war, the baseball owners started what they called the All-American Girls Professional Baseball League. After the war the AAGPBL continued play until the mid 1950s, and two days after she graduated from high school, Jackie started traveling around the country with the Grand Rapids Chicks. In '49 and '50 she played second base, and she loved every minute of it. She was independent and adventurous, and Kate has a lot of Jackie in her.

"Listen, Kate," I said. "You know those letters I told you about? The ones I said you couldn't read unless something happened to me?"

"I remember," she said.

"Well, in yours I say, 'Be careful,' and it's not because I don't trust you but because I know you."

"You know what?" she said with that sheepish grin of hers.

"Don't play that game with me," I said. "I checked out the pictures on the Noah's Ark website. I know that last summer you went glacier sliding on your back down Mount Shavano, and I know you went midnight rafting with what's-his-name earlier in the summer when the water was deep and fast, and I know that when a kid in your raft lost his paddle, you went in after it and almost drowned."

"I didn't almost drown." She rolled her eyes. "I just got stuck in the body slot for a minute or two. It was no big deal."

"Look," I said, "anytime you're stuck between two rocks in the middle of the river and the water is washing over your head, trust me, it's a big deal! God himself was watching out for you that day and you know it, so don't go telling me it was no big deal."

"Okay, Dad," she said. "I get it. I'll be careful, I promise."

For a few minutes the two of us sat there in silence, staring at our shoes. I wanted to hug her and hold her, but I was cautious because Kate doles out affection sparingly. "I love you, Kate," I said in a low, steady voice. "I know it makes you uncomfortable to talk about it, but I love you with all my heart. In fact, you are my heart, and I couldn't stand the thought of anything ever happening to you. You know that, right?"

"I know, Dad," she said softly. "I love you too." She reached over and gave me a hug around the neck. "Now get out of this truck and let me get going before we start crying like a couple of girls," she said, pulling her emotions back together again.

"You are a girl, Kate," I said, smiling as I got out of the car.

"And you are too, Dad." She grinned impishly. "I'll call you when I get to Kearney," she said, and then she pulled out of the driveway, waving and calling, "Love ya, Dad!"

"Love you too!" I shouted, but I'm not sure she heard me.

Prodigals have a way of taking your heart with them when they go. And when she came home again that fall I wanted to yell, "Get a robe and a ring and kill the fatted calf!" but I didn't. I just whispered a prayer of gratitude and then said, "Let's go out to Vitale's for pizza."

For Tara, the letter day was her wedding day. That was an emotional day for me on many levels. I was so happy that she and Adam were getting married and so sad that my mom could not be there to see it. Knowing that Mom loved butterflies, Carol, her twin sister Cheryl, and Tara had spent hours making hundreds of them out of colored tissue paper and cardboard and hanging them in the trees along the beach walk at Camp Willows where Tara was going to be married. The day of her wedding, as she and I were about to make our way down the beach walkway toward the outdoor chapel, I shared some thoughts from her letter. She and I had always shared a love of art and beauty. When we went on family vacations, the two of us would sometimes take a day trip to visit the art museums in places like Chicago; Washington, DC; Sarasota; and Detroit. After one of those trips, I wrote a few lines about the sketches she'd made and added them to her letter later that year.

"You see what others miss," I wrote. "While others admired the misty colors of Claude Monet, you sketched the old woman sitting on the bench on the edge of the gallery. When everyone else was gazing at the sculpture by Alexander Calder, you drew the little boy in the crowd watching the ducks on the pond nearby as he held tightly to his mother's hand. At the Chihuly exhibit, as art critics and amateurs gasped in awe at the beauty of the blown glass, you captured the sadness in the tired old eyes of the janitor who leaned against his broom handle at the end of a long day. Sweet Tara, you love beautiful things, but you love people more, and I love you for it."

I held her hands, looked into her eyes, and said, "Thank you, Tara."

"For what?" she asked.

"The butterflies," I said. "They're for me, aren't they?"

"Yes," she said. "And for me."

As the music began to play, we made our way down the sidewalk, crying bittersweet tears of joy as butterflies danced in the breeze along the tree-lined path. After giving her hand to Adam, I sat on the bench next to Carol, and then, right on cue, the most beautiful monarch butterfly landed on the cement a few feet in front of me. I looked at Carol and she nodded. No words were necessary. We both were thinking the same thing: my mom was letting us know that she was there. My heart almost beat out of my chest as the butterfly sat motionless until the preacher pronounced Adam and Tara husband and wife. Then, as Adam kissed his bride, the butterfly gently flapped her wings and flew away.

Each generation stands on the shoulders of those who've gone before them.

I never prayed that their lives would be easy, or happy, or trouble free. I prayed that they would be faithful and fulfilled, that they would make a difference in the lives of the people around them, and that they'd feel like they were a part of something bigger than themselves. Graciously, God answered my prayers.

Our girls are grown women now. They each have learned the lessons we taught them about faith and life and family. Now it's their turn to become teachers. That's how it works. Hopefully they'll do a better job than I did, but each generation stands on the shoulders of those who've gone before them.

forgiveness

"I can forgive, but I cannot forget," is only another way of saying, "I will not forgive."

Henry Ward Beecher

8

I was so lost in thought that I didn't even hear her come in. "Would you like a piece of pie, honey?" she asked, and even though the light was dim, I knew it was her. She was young, beautiful, and in some ways unrecognizable to me. I didn't know her when she was a young woman, but I knew the sound of her voice, the smile on her face, and the sparkle in her eyes. For as long as I could remember, she'd looked the same as she did in the picture on the bookcase at my folks' house.

Her hair was a bluish shade of white, and it was pulled back in a bun. Her glasses were thick, her makeup was a little caked, and she wore faux pearl earrings the size of quarters. When she slept, she kept her teeth in a jar on the nightstand next to her glasses, and when she was awake, she always wore a dress, nylons, and sturdy black shoes with low-wedged heels.

My kids always called her Grandma Great Kate, and she was the kindest, gentlest soul I'd ever known. Grandpa, on the other hand, was another story. The whiskey would have its way with him, and then he'd have his way with Grandma. He let her know who was the boss, sometimes physically but always verbally. He did the same thing with his kids too, but when he'd start in on them, Grandma would step between them, and usually she'd end up with a black eye or a fat lip for her troubles.

Once my wife asked her how long she was married before she knew she'd made a mistake. Grandma Great Kate said that she knew the day after she said "I do," but people didn't get divorced in those days, so she tried to make the best of it. Grandma lived to be one hundred and nine, a full twenty years past Grandpa, and we all figured that God was trying to make it up to her.

My uncle Herb told me once that after my dad had come home from World War II, he'd gone over to see Grandma and found her sitting on the back porch nursing a black eye. Grandpa was in the backyard, and Dad went out there, grabbed him by the shirt, dragged him out behind the garage, and beat the tar out of him.

Then, as Grandpa lay bleeding on the ground, my dad shouted, "If I ever hear that you hurt her again, I'm going to come back and finish what I started, and when I do, I'll bury you next to those rosebushes, and no one will miss you! Do you hear me, old man?"

His words were harsh. He treated Grandpa like Grandpa treated everyone else. There was no grace in his words. It was an eye for an eye and a tooth for a tooth, but sometimes God expects us to defend the innocent and the helpless, and this was one of those times. After that, Grandpa never hurt Grandma again, not physically anyway.

There are times when God expects us to defend the innocent and the helpless.

Now Grandma asked me, "Did you want cherry or lemon?" Before I could answer, she shook her head. "Oh, what am I thinking? I know perfectly well that lemon is your favorite and Sharon and Ben always preferred the cherry."

I never met a pie I didn't like, but for some reason Grandma got it in her head that I liked lemon better, and I never saw any reason to correct her. Besides, when she'd start baking, she always made an extra little lemon pie for me, and I figured there was no reason to mess with a good thing.

When she brought me my piece of pie, she also brought a deck of cards. Grandma loved to play cards and talk, so that's what we did. We talked about her mom and dad and how they'd come over on the boat from the Netherlands. They'd had fourteen kids; one of them died young, but all the others lived well into their nineties or hundreds.

"How's Mina?" she asked. Mina was her youngest sister.

"Mina's great," I answered. "She just turned one hundred."

"I know," she said. "You should go visit her sometime."

"I know," I replied, feeling a little guilty that I hadn't.

Her father, Great-Grandpa Vanden Bout, was a wooden shoe maker in the old country, and when he came to America, he worked six days a week in the furniture factory and as a janitor in the old Dutch church on nights and weekends. In the only picture I ever saw of him, he was sitting proud as a peacock with his wife and their thirteen children. He wore a suit and spats and had a full head of flowing white hair, which made him look more like the governor than the church janitor.

It's a parent's job to give their children the chance to live a better life.

When I asked why he came to this country, Great-Grandpa Vanden Bout said, "My grandfather, my father, and I were all wooden shoe makers, and if I didn't come to this country, you too would be a wooden shoe maker."

Great-Grandpa Vanden Bout believed that it was a parent's job to give his children the chance to live a better life.

"He would be so proud of you," Grandma Kate said, reading my thoughts. "The wooden shoe maker's great-grandson, a doctor. Who could imagine such a thing!" It humbled me to hear her say it. I only hoped I could have the dignity and character that he had.

"Will I get to see him?" I asked.

"Not this time," she responded, "but sometime soon, perhaps. No one knows for sure."

"By the way, how's little Kate?" she asked. Kate is my oldest daughter and her namesake. Then she asked about Kelly and Tara, my wife, Sharon and Ben, and my cousins, and I asked her about Uncle Ernie, and Frank, and John, and Nettie. Then I asked her if she knew where Grandpa was.

"Oh," she replied. "He's here, and I'm glad for him."

Forgiveness is simply deciding to stop letting the hurt of yesterday pollute and poison today.

"Well, first off," I said, "I guess I'm a little surprised to hear that he made it, but then I'm even more surprised that you're glad about it."

"I don't blame him," she said. "It was what he learned as a child. People who hurt people were once hurt by people themselves. It goes back for generations. It's a vicious cycle, it's part of the conspiracy, and the only thing that breaks it is love. Your dad, your aunt and uncle, and I—we all tried as best we could to love the anger out of him, and on those days when we couldn't love him, we loved each other. Besides, don't you remember that God broke Grandpa's stone-hard heart right before he died, and he gave his heart to Jesus? It's never too late for that," she said. "Never! There's always room for forgiveness."

Grandma Kate had often said, "Our sins are written in pencil, but our forgiveness is written in ink." Forgiveness came natural to her. In the book of Romans, Paul once wrote, "If it's possible, as far as it depends on you, live at peace with everyone." Grandma did that. She believed that just as God had forgiven her, it was her job to forgive others, even Grandpa. Not that her forgiveness justified his actions, because it didn't. She wasn't saying that what he did was all right or acceptable, and she certainly wasn't giving trust where trust was not deserved. She was simply granting mercy where mercy was not deserved, and in her mind that's what God would expect. Each time she forgave Grandpa, she was not letting him off the hook for what he'd done, but she was letting herself off the hook for what he'd done to her.

"You see," she'd say, "forgiveness is about us, not them. When we forgive someone, we're releasing ourselves from the prison of the past. Forgiveness is simply deciding to stop letting the hurt of yesterday pollute and poison today."

I can remember Grandma saying, "Forgiveness is a choice; it's always a choice, and if we refuse to forgive, then bitterness, resentment, and hatred fill our hearts with an all-consuming desire for revenge. That's no way to live, and so we have no choice but to forgive."

Whenever we'd say good-bye to an aging Grandma Kate, she'd hold up her twisted arthritic hand as if to say, "Come, hold my hand, and give your Grandma a kiss good-bye." Then, when I'd bend down, she would pull me close and say, "Now you pray that I wake up in heaven. Your dad can't do that, he's not ready to say good-bye, but you're stronger, and I'm ready now, so you pray."

Afterward she'd give me a peppermint to seal the deal. Her peppermints always tasted a little like perfume because they'd been rolling around in her purse for weeks.

I did what she asked. I'd pray that God would take her gently in the night, but I always felt a little guilty about it because God knew my heart wasn't in it. I knew that I'd miss her too; I just didn't know how much.

Love and forgiveness are always a choice.

But seeing her today . . . it was different. I was glad I helped pray her into heaven. She'd given up that old bent body of hers and taken on a new body—young, strong, and beautiful.

Now instead of me leaving Grandma Kate, she was leaving me. She got up, walked over to me, and said what I always said to her: "Don't get up, I'll find my way out. You just sit." Then she bent low, kissed me good-bye, and said, "This is what I have for you: *Love and forgiveness are a choice.* They're always a choice, so choose wisely."

"That's it?" I asked.

"That's it," she replied. "That's it—choose wisely because the choices you make reflect your heart." She handed me a peppermint as she walked out the door.

I watched through the window as she walked down the driveway and into the darkness. As I sat there sucking the perfume off the peppermint, I remembered that Grandma never did learn how to drive.

As her silhouette faded into the darkness, I sat down on the couch in front of the fireplace, and my mind drifted back to the time we were all down by the swimming docks at Stony Lake. It was over forty years ago—I was about sixteen, Ben was eleven, and my two cousins, Steve and Dave, were eight and six.

I was knee deep in the water, about to go water-skiing, and Grandma Great Kate had walked out on the dock to watch. She was well into her seventies, and as usual, she was wearing those granny heels and a house dress. Dad and Uncle Herb had just come in from bass fishing—in fact, Dad had caught a big one off of someplace called Promise Point—and they walked up to show off their catch to Mom and Aunt Gerry, who were sunbathing on the beach.

Ben, Dave, and Steve jumped in off the end of the dock, and when Grandma heard the splash, she turned, ran toward the sound, and dove in, headfirst, to save them. In an instant Dad and Uncle Herb got up, raced down the dock, and dove in to save her. By the time I got there, they all had come up, with their heads bouncing like bobbers in the water.

"What the heck did you think you were doing?" Dad yelled to Grandma Kate.

"I didn't know the boys could swim," she answered with a smile.

"Well," Dad replied, "then I guess we're even. We didn't know you could swim either."

Whenever Dad would tell the story, he'd always say, "Greater love hath no one than that they would lay down their life for another."

Grandma always had peanut butter cookies that bore the marks of being pressed with a fork, always had Dutch Babbelaars that had started to turn back to brown sugar again, and always had time for you. Whatever she was doing would be set aside as soon as anyone came to call. Nothing was more important to her than the people she loved, and she let you know it.

As the fire dwindled into embers, I said my prayers and went off to bed. That night, for the first time in a long time, I asked for nothing but the wisdom to know how blessed my life has been.

potential

Everyone has inside of him a piece of good news. The good news is you don't know how great you can be! How much you can love! What you can accomplish! And what your potential is!

Anne Frank

9

I woke to the smell of something wonderful, and when I went downstairs, Ahbee was pulling little spinach and artichoke soufflés out of the oven. He set two of them on a plate with some sliced strawberries and handed it to me along with a glass of freshly squeezed orange juice.

"Have a seat, Scout," he said. "Looks like you'll be spending the day with me today."

There was something about him that both put me at ease and made me uncomfortable. There was a warmth in his voice and appearance and a tenderness in his eyes. I felt confident that he cared about me, but being in his presence was also intimidating. It's hard to explain, but I felt small in his presence. Like when I did something wrong as a kid and I'd have to sit on the naughty chair and wait for my dad to come home. I knew it was going to go one of two ways: I was either going to get a licking or a lecture. The licking was painful but quick, and so I much preferred it to the alternative.

When Dad would lecture me he'd take his time. He'd start with the look. He'd get this pained expression on his face that said, "You've really let me down on this one, Sky. I'm so disappointed.

We talked about this before, and I expect more from you than that." The longer he'd wait to speak, the smaller I'd feel. And then when he did speak, it wasn't so much what he said but how he said it—slow, deliberate, almost in a whisper so you'd have to strain to hear him. He said it in such a way that you knew it pained him to have to talk about it.

One of the only times I ever saw my dad cry was when I got caught changing a grade on my report card. Dad had said that if I didn't get my English grade up, I wasn't going to be able to go on a fishing trip we had planned in Canada. I promised I would, but I didn't. So as I rode home from school on the bus, I took out my report card and a ball-point pen and changed an F to a B. But when the teacher called my house a few days later, my trickery was exposed.

"How could you do that?" Dad said. "They could tell me my boy wasn't trying, they could tell me that you just weren't able to understand, and I'd have believed them. But when they told me you were a cheat, that you lied to me, I said no way, not Sky, he'd never lie to me." And then a tear rolled down his cheek. I remember feeling tiny when he said that, insignificant, like I'd let him down and there was nothing I could ever do to make it right. In a word, I felt guilty.

That's how I felt around Ahbee. I felt little, and unworthy, and exposed. Like he could see the secrets I kept hidden in my soul. It was unnerving, especially when it was quiet, so I tried to keep the conversation going. We exchanged words about the weather and the way the water was rippling across the lake, but he didn't seem to be in much of a mood for conversation. So mostly I just sat there feeling small in the uncomfortable silence.

After we were done with breakfast, Ahbee asked me if I was ready.

"Ready for what?" I asked.

"You and I are going to talk about what you've learned in the last couple of days," he answered. "It's a lot of information to digest."

Ahbee was right. I'd been through a lot in the last few days, and I hadn't really taken the time to digest much of what I'd learned. Even the day I took a walk by myself had been a learning experience. I'd relived some of the accident, and I knew that at least some of the lessons I'd learned here had something to do with that. There was a part of me that was ready to forgive myself for my part in it all, but there was still so much I wanted to know. Spending some time with Ahbee was exactly what I wanted to do, but I also felt like I needed to clear the air.

"I'm sorry for what I said down by the creek. I didn't mean it. It was just so painful for me to remember."

"It was painful for me too," Ahbee said. "But sometimes pain is necessary." With that, he walked out the door.

"Well, are you coming?" he asked as he walked out back toward the carriage house.

"Right behind you."

It was a beautiful day. The sun was shining, and the sky was filled with those big, cotton-like clouds that seemed to roll across the horizon.

Ahbee opened the garage door and got into the driver's seat of a cream-colored '67 Volvo 122s station wagon. It had red-ribbed leather interior, gray carpet, and big, black rubber mud mats. I took the shotgun seat on the passenger's side, we both clicked on the three-point seatbelts, and as soon as Ahbee turned the key, the little four-cylinder motor responded with a gentle purr.

The car was kind of a throwback. It had an AM radio and crank windows, and the gauges were round and retro, black-faced with white letters. The steering wheel was gigantic, speaking to the fact that the car did not have power steering, but the thing that stuck out most to me was the length of the throw on the stick transmission. Like the shift lever itself, it was awkwardly long, and when Ahbee put it in reverse, he banged my knee.

We drove along a winding road in silence for about twenty minutes before I asked where we were going.

"No place in particular," Ahbee replied, rolling down the window. "Sometimes I just find it helpful to take a ride. There's something freeing about driving this stretch of road and listening to the sound of the tires on the pavement."

The scope of heaven is much grander than we can imagine.

I had to agree. The road chased the coastline, winding its way through dense woods that tumbled up against the side of a snow-capped mountain. The terrain seemed to be a mixture of all of my favorite places. At times the coastline was rocky and dropped off several hundred feet from the narrow shoulder of the road. Other times there were woods out both windows, and then a little farther on, the road would open up to a panoramic vista as it ran along the coast flanked by the low bluff of a rolling sand dune.

The water was blue and clear, and finally I asked, "Is that the ocean?"

Ahbee answered, "No, not exactly. It's the Crystal Sea."

Of course it is, I thought to myself. *I should have known that. If this is heaven, then what else could it be?*

"It could be lots of things," Ahbee said, answering the question I never asked. "The scope of heaven is much grander than you imagine—oceans, rivers, mountains, deserts, rain forests, glacial tundras, magnificent cities."

"Cities?"

"Of course! Shops, theaters, restaurants . . . whatever you've enjoyed in your world is but a taste of mine. You have no idea the things that I have imagined, and when I think of something, it is."

"Just like that?" I asked.

"If by 'that' you mean in that very moment in terms of time as you know it, then I would say no. Remember, I'm not bound by time."

Ahbee continued, "To me a day is like a thousand years, and a thousand years is like the blink of an eye. Time and all its limitations and anxiety are a result of Adam's indiscretion. The Fallen One is in charge of calendars, the aging process, and death and deadlines of any kind. You'll notice that I wear no wristwatch."

Up until that moment, I actually hadn't noticed. In fact, I'm sure that I probably hadn't noticed a lot of things, but since there were no hands on the clock in the kitchen, I shouldn't have been surprised.

"You're right," Ahbee said, again reading my thoughts. "That's what this little car ride is all about. You see, at some point you're going back to your world again, and when you do, I want you to share a little bit of what you've learned here.

"Like Moses, the prophets, and the others, you've been chosen. You've been sent out ahead of the others so that you can go back and tell them what's waiting for them just over the horizon. You've been brought here so that you can go back there and give them a report. Every generation has its prophets, you know.

"Unfortunately, the Fallen One has found a way to cut the lives of most of them short. Their heightened sensitivity to all things spiritual made them targets. I don't want you to take this wrong, but to be honest, that's why we've chosen you. At times you've been an unwilling part of the conspiracy, and so you'll have credibility on both sides."

God often uses unlikely prophets to share his heart.

To be honest, I wasn't sure if I should be honored for being mentioned in the company of men like Moses or offended for being accused of sometimes siding with evil, but I sat mute because I knew it was true. I've spent some time in both camps. Ahbee nodded as if he'd read my thoughts, then continued.

"Others have claimed to speak in my name with threatening rage and hellfire judgment or a smooth and easy promise, and they've captured people's attention by telling them what they wanted to hear. But for the most part, you've sat comfortably on the fence. You're wonderfully average, a mediocre Christian tucked comfortably out of the limelight and off the Fallen One's radar, and so you're as an unlikely a prophet as I could find. He'd never suspect that we'd choose to use someone like you, and that's the beauty of it."

"But I'm a psychologist, not a preacher," I said. "Any teaching I do is merely a sideline—a class or two at the college, some Sunday school sometimes."

"Exactly my point," Ahbee responded. "We've had our eye on you for a long time. You've managed to elude the temptation to compromise the truth, but at the same time you've never proclaimed it with enough conviction to attract attention to yourself. Ordinarily, when someone is neither hot nor cold, they are of very little use to me, but in this case, you're perfect."

Our potential is only as limited as our dreams.

Imagine that, I thought to myself. *God thinks I'm perfect!* Of course, I wasn't sure if he intended that to be a compliment, but I took it as one. Besides, being labeled as an unlikely prophet put me in pretty good company—Jonah, Moses, Gideon, David, and Paul. None of them were professional preachers, and at one point, they were all as unlikely a candidate as I to be the messengers of the Most High.

"Is that what Roz meant when he said that you weren't done with me yet?" I asked.

"That's a part of it," Ahbee replied. "You have a wealth of potential hidden inside you. Of course, I believe that about everyone, so I'm no more done with anyone else than I am with you. Each of you is born with a lifetime's supply of mulligans, second chances, and do-overs in your birth package. Unfortunately, you give up on yourselves when I have never given up on you."

His blue eyes flashed as he began to explain. "Each day you're given a new chance to become the person I created you to be. Your potential is only as limited as your dreams. Children understand that. That's why they have such huge, bodacious dreams. They haven't learned to limit their possibilities yet, and so each night they go to sleep dreaming about how they're going to change the world, and every day they begin a new adventure.

"But as you get older, you settle. You trade your big dreams for little dreams. Instead of changing the world, you dream about changing jobs, or changing your address, or changing the way you wear your hair. The problem is that I have planted eternity in your hearts. I have sown the seeds of greatness in your souls, and so naturally when you settle for anything less, it's not very satisfying. Does that make sense to you?" Ahbee asked.

We were made for so much more than most of us settle for.

"It makes perfect sense," I replied. "It's what I've always thought Solomon was trying to say when he said that all of life was meaningless, but until now, I was never quite sure."

"Be sure!" Ahbee responded. "Be very sure!"

I nodded as if to agree, but really I was only on the cusp of understanding. Little by little I shuffled his words through my mind like a deck of cards, and one by one the pieces began falling into place. So many of the things that I thought would make me happy in life in fact did quite the opposite, and now I understood why. We were made for so much more than most of us settle for.

"Let me ask you something," Ahbee said. "Do you ever miss the car business?"

It was a question I'd been asked a lot in my life. "Not much," I said. "I miss driving a different car home every night, and the dealer trips, and some of the people. Some of my closest friends and family are still in the car business. But I guess what I miss the most is feeling like I was in control. I felt invincible in those days, like there wasn't anything I couldn't fix."

"The invincibility is part of the ignorance of youth," Ahbee said. "Eventually you outgrow it. But the need to be in control, the desire to fix everything—it's your Achilles' heel."

He was right. I'm a fixer, always have been, and never has that been more true than when it came to Ben.

After he dropped out of college, for the next several months Ben hung around the dealership, did some odd jobs, worked a little in the wash bay, and drove the parts truck. In those days Ben was running with a wild crew. They drank too much and did a little dope, and his life was skidding in a downward spiral. On Friday nights I gave him a little extra cash to wash down the shop floors. It was kind of a stupid-proof job. You'd just wet the floor down with a hose, sprinkle an industrial-size box of Tide all over, and scrub the grease and oil stains with a firm-bristle shop broom. Then you'd rinse it down, turn the shop fans on, and you were done. Alone it took him about four hours, but it could be a little boring, so sometimes he'd invite a friend to help and then pay him something under the table.

One night he'd asked Brian to help him, and that kid was trouble. He'd played high school football with Ben, and it was the high-water mark of his life. He was forever saying things like, "Remember the game against East when you threw me that touchdown pass in the last five minutes of the last quarter?" Of course Ben remembered. It was like Ben's whole football career was on a tape in his head, and it didn't take much from Brian to get him to hit PLAY. I just didn't think it was what he needed, especially in light of the accident.

Brian worked part-time at the convenience store, mostly, I think, so he could sneak beer out the back door, and otherwise he hung out at the pool hall. Brian got the bright idea that they could get the keys to the Dodge Power Wagon we used for plowing and go mud running. For some reason it sounded like a good idea to Ben too, probably because they'd been drinking beers while they washed the floors, and around quarter to ten the two of them were headed out to the swamp. After about three hours of "Ya-hoos" and "Watch this!" they caromed off a tree and ended up buried in mud halfway up the doors, and that's when Ben called me.

I was mad because he called and woke up my family, I was mad because he took the truck without asking, but mostly I was mad because I felt like Ben's life was self-destructing on my watch, and I didn't know what to do about it.

I ragged on him on the phone for a while, and then, like always, I fixed it. I sent Earl's Towing out to get the two of them and the truck. I let it sit for the weekend, and then on Monday I called him into my office for a little talk.

"Look, Ben," I said. "I don't really care about the stupid Power Wagon, but I do care about you. If it were up to me, you'd go back to college. If money is a problem, I can help—really, I'm glad to help. Call it a loan. You can pay me back whenever. Never, for all I care."

"I appreciate that, bro," Ben said. "But the only reason to go to college was football, and that's done now. Maybe someday I'll be ready for that, but not now, not for a long time."

"Well, you've got to do something," I said. "You can't just hang around with Brian and get wasted on weekends."

"I know," he said, "and I've been thinking about that too. I think I want to work here with you and Gary." He said that Tom Dykstra was going to quit and go into the insurance business with his brother, and he'd like to take his job. Tom sold new cars, mostly VWs.

When Ben asked, what could I say? If Ben wanted to sell cars, how could I say no? I owed him. When I talked to Al and Gary about it, they said, "Of course, he's family, and he'd be a great fit."

Ben took to selling cars like he took to football. He was a natural. Six months later he was our top salesman, and he and Al were two sides of the same coin. They both lived full tilt. Run and gun. Work hard, play hard.

"The kid's got moxie," Al said, "and he's cool under pressure. I think maybe we need to give him a shot at taking Gordy's place in used cars."

Gordy had been our used car manager, and although Al liked him, he and I never got along. I always felt like he had his hand in my pocket. It seemed to me like he was wholesaling off some of the cream, but we were making money, so Al was happy. Even so, it didn't feel right to me. Then one day Gordy had Cal Weelers from Cal's Fine Cars and Fred Keenan from Keenan Car Company going in a bidding war on a Buick convertible, and when Keenan lost he wasn't too happy with Gordy.

He came in my office and said, "Rooster"—Fred always called me Rooster because I dressed a little flashy in those days—"I thought you ought to know that Gordy's getting a fifty under the table every time he wholesales a car. I've paid it plenty, but I never felt good about it, it's always kind of stuck in my craw, so now I'm telling you." Then he leaned over, spit a wad of chewing tobacco into my wastebasket, and said, "Yes sir, that's a fact!"

Fred was a lot of things, but he'd always been straight with me. I thanked him for coming clean, and when he left I called Cal, and he confirmed what Fred had said.

I walked over to the used car lot, called Gordy out on it, and fired him right there on the spot.

"Listen, kid," he said, "it's part of the business, everybody does it, and besides, I don't work for you, I work for Al."

"I don't care if everybody does it," I said. "We don't do it, and if you don't get off this lot right now, I'm going to throw you off."

For a minute we stared at each other like two bull moose ready to square off, but then Gordy backed down. He left in a huff and called Al when he got home, but Al backed my play.

For the next few months I was busier than I wanted to be, trying to cover for Gordy being gone. I was doing the ordering, checking the deals, appraising the trades, and trying to buy a few cars at the auction, and little things started falling through the cracks. One day Al came in my office and said, "Look, I get it, you wanted to fire Gordy, but we need somebody going to the auction." That's when he told me to give Ben a shot at it.

"He's awful young," I said.

"Not any younger than you were when I started bringing you there," he said.

So, reluctantly, I started taking Ben with me when I went on Fridays, and he picked it up pretty fast. The car auction is every auction you've ever seen, on steroids. It's sixteen lanes of cars all being bid on at the same time, with crowds of people yelling, nodding, winking, talking, and eating. It's nothing short of organized pandemonium.

Outside there are four or five hundred cars, each with a run number and the mileage printed on a card hanging from the mirror. For example, if the card said "82K, D-17," that meant it had 82 thousand miles on it and would be the seventeenth car to run through lane D.

The dealers get there a couple hours before the auction opens to look over the inventory and write down the numbers of the cars they want to bid on. Afterward they stand around and trade stories. It's kind of fun in the summer, but along about February it can be brutal. You go out, brush off the ones you're interested in, and hope the snow and ice doesn't hide something. It's a rite of passage. Every one of us has been hurt a time or two, but you learn what to look for. Ordinarily it's kind of a good ol' boys' club, and the old-timers will take advantage of a new face, but a couple of them took to Ben right away, and within a few weeks he was in.

You've got to be registered as a dealer to get in the place. It's not open to the public. Everyone is required to wear a badge with your name and the dealership's name on it, and anyone who's wearing a badge can bid.

Once I brought my daughter Tara to one, and when the auctioneer nodded at her, she politely nodded back. Back and forth it went. He nodded and she nodded until he slammed the gavel down and yelled, "Sold to the young lady in the blue coat—is she with you, Sky?"

I said, "She is," and then I told her not to nod at anyone but me for the rest of the day.

I never had that problem with Ben. He knew what he wanted to buy and what he was willing to pay, and he usually left the auction with what he wanted. Some guys just have a knack for it, and Ben was one of them.

The last time Ben and I went to the auction was when I got my Outback. I used to go more often, partly to be with Ben and partly to keep an eye on him, but lately I'd been too busy. Besides, sometimes I'm better off not knowing. I know full well the dark side of humanity, but rarely is it on display in such proportion as it is at a car auction. You might think there would be a kind of honor among thieves, so to speak, but you'd be wrong.

A few years ago on a cold January morning, Ben and I were walking the back lot at the auction prior to the sale to see if there was something we wanted to bid on. I spotted an older Subaru wagon that I thought might be a good car for Kate to drive to college. It had some miles on it but otherwise looked to be in good shape. I got in the driver's seat and tried to start it, but it had a dead battery. I said to Ben that if we could get a jump, I'd like to take the car for a test drive.

"No need," he said. "It's junk."

"How do you know it's junk?" I said. "You haven't even heard it run."

"Don't need to," he said. "It's got bad valves."

"And how do you know that?" I asked.

"Look, bro," he said. "Let me take you to school. Come on, follow me." He turned and walked inside where Jim Fisher from Quality Cars was standing. We exchanged greetings and made a little small talk. I used to wholesale Jim some cars when I was more involved in the dealership.

Then Ben said, "Say, Jim, if you saw an older Subaru out on the lot with 125K on it and the battery was dead, what would you think?"

"I'd think it had bad valves," he said.

"Me too," Ben said. "Me too. Cold valves are quiet valves." Then he and Jim laughed. Later he explained to me that the guy selling it intentionally left the key on when he parked it to run the battery down so you couldn't pre-drive it and warm it up.

"You're just too trusting, Sky," he said. "Remember that Baptist preacher with the 220D?"

"I remember," I said.

"Well, if you can't trust a Baptist preacher, what makes you think you can trust a bunch of used car dealers?"

Back in the day, this Baptist preacher came in and wanted to buy a used Audi we had on the lot, and he had this old 220 Mercedes diesel he wanted to trade in with 106 thousand miles on it. We went back and forth on price a little, but eventually we put a deal together taking the 220 in on trade. It had a few dings and a chip in the windshield, and it was barefoot, which is to say the tires were bald, but it ran great, so we sent it out to be cleaned and painted and serviced and put it on the lot. A couple weeks later a guy named Charlie came in and wanted to buy it really cheap, so we sold it to him "as is," which is to say with no warranty.

We didn't hear from him again for a couple of months, but then one day Charlie came marching in my office all red-faced with his attorney in tow, demanding his money back. He called me a cheat and a liar and threatened to sue.

I got up, closed the door to my office, and said, "Calm down, Charlie. Why don't you just tell me what this is all about?"

He jaw-jacked me a while, and then he said that the 220 was burning some oil, and when he took it over to German Auto Werks they recognized the car. They checked their service records and said that it had 206 thousand miles on it, not 106. He then said he called the Baptist preacher and he confirmed it.

"Hold on a minute, Charlie," I said. "Let me check the file." When I checked, I had an odometer affidavit signed by the good pastor, and it clearly said 106,042 miles on it.

"Well, somebody's lying," Charlie said, "and I want my money back! And I expect to be reimbursed for what German Auto Werks charged me too."

"And you'll get it," I said. "But first you've got to help me nail that lying Baptist, okay?"

He looked at his attorney, and after he gave him the nod, Charlie said, "Sounds like fun to me," and the game was on. I hooked up a tape recorder to my phone and had Charlie call the preacher again to confirm that the 220 really had two hundred thousand on it when he traded it in. He must have smelled that something was fishy, so he was reluctant at first, but Charlie kept after him, God bless him, and finally he got him to say it. Then I grabbed the phone and said, "I've got you now, preacher! Either you bring me a check for what I just paid ol' Charlie here, or I'm going to call Channel 4 tomorrow and expose you for what you are." Then I hung up, feeling quite proud of myself.

The next day I got a phone call from the preacher's attorney informing me that they would not be bringing us a check, and in fact they were suing us for slander.

"Sue all you want," I said, "but I've got your client on tape."

"Yes, well, that may never make it into court," he said. "And even if it does, it'll be a while. We're prepared to drag this out for a long, long time, and meanwhile I've asked the judge to put a gag order on this. You won't be able to say a word to the media, and with the recent litigation involving Cascade Cadillac, who do you think is going to look bad when it gets out that you, a car dealer, and my client, a well-respected Baptist minister, are going to court over an odometer dispute? If I were you, I'd check with your attorney before you do anything stupid." And then he hung up.

I was so mad I could spit. Immediately I called Dirk Hathorne of Hathorne, Hathorne, and DeJong.

"I want this Bible thumper's head on a plate," I said. "The bloodier the better. I want him to hurt."

"Hold on," said Dirk. "You better explain what you're talking about." When I did he said, "His attorney is right. You can't ignore a gag order, and I know this guy, he's good, he'll drag it out for a year or two, and meanwhile it'll cost you guys a lot of business."

"I don't care what it costs," I said. "I want to brand that sucker. I don't want his money, I want his reputation."

"That may be," Dirk said, "but you'll spend more with me than the car is worth. If I were you I'd be thinking less about what this could do to his reputation and more about what it could do to yours. Maybe you'd better talk to Al before you do something stupid."

He was right and I knew it, but hearing him say it pricked my balloon. "You may be right," I said, "but it isn't fair."

"Who ever said the law was fair?" Dirk said. "Call me tomorrow and let me know what you want to do." With that he hung up.

I talked to Al, and eventually we decided the best thing was just to cut our losses, and that's what we did. I wanted to go slash the guy's tires or superglue his door locks, but I didn't. I went back to selling cars and he went back to preaching, and I took some comfort in the fact that someday we'd both have to answer for what we did.

———

Here it is: there are crooks in any business, but most car dealers I know are pretty straight. I'm not saying they're choirboys, but they're not turning speedometers back or packing bad transmissions with bananas to keep them quiet. That stuff went out with AM radios and whitewall tires. But when it comes down to feeding their families, sometimes they stick their toe over the line. And that's where Ben was.

Mary Alice, Ben's ex, spent money like they were printing it in the garage, and neither one of them was willing to live on a budget. It was like a contest. If Ben spent money on something like a battery for the lawn tractor, she'd go out and spend an equal amount or more on something she wanted.

Ben was having one of those kinds of months when he sold the five-speed that wasn't. It was August, and the new models were coming out in a few weeks. We had some of last year's models in stock, but we'd spiffed them, which is to say we paid an extra two hundred dollars to the salesman for every one he rolled, and they were going fast. Ben had a customer who wanted a rojo red two-door Rabbit, but it had to be a five-speed, and they were hard to get. The rule in the car business is that when you can't sell them what they want, you sell them something you can get. It's called a flip, and Ben was good at it, especially with women. He'd flash that million-dollar grin of his, give a little wink, and before they knew what happened he'd have moved them from a two-door to a four-door, or from a red one to a green one, or in this case, from a five-speed to a four-speed. So he walked her through a buy like we had a basement full of red five-speeds.

He had me appraise her trade, told her five-speeds cost more and didn't really get that much better mileage, and tried to move her to a four-speed on the floor. But she wouldn't budge. Her boyfriend had told her that *Road and Track* tested the five-speed and said it was faster and smoother, and with a lot of highway driving it would pay for itself. Ben tried everything, but she just kept saying, "My boyfriend says . . ."

Finally he wrote her up for what she wanted and took a deposit. Of course Ben knew we didn't have a chance of getting one, but he also knew that the more people she told that she'd just bought a new car, the harder it would be for her to back out when and if he had to flip her.

We searched the locator, but the only one for five hundred miles was Jim Morran's demo. Jim was on vacation, but he was coming home on Friday, the 29th, so Ben decided he'd flip her into that.

He called her in, explained the situation, and after a little banter, he wrote it up for three hundred less than their original deal and told her she could pick it up on Saturday the 30th.

The problem was that somebody's grandma backed her Buick into the side of Jim's demo while they were camping at the state park, and when Ben pulled in on Friday, his heart sank. He needed that car to make his month, but he also needed more than a day to pull out the fender, put a new door skin on it, and get it painted. He called Larry the body shop manager, but he said there was no way to do all that by Saturday morning. That's when Ben put his toe over the line again.

He called back to Donny in the wash bay, told him to go over to the parts department, get a five-speed shift knob, put it on the red two-door demo that Mary Alice had been driving, and get the car cleaned up for delivery. The car was a twin to Jim's except it had premium sound, a couple thousand less miles, and a four-speed.

On Saturday, paperwork-wise he sold her Jim's demo, but he delivered Mary Alice's. He told the customer that the radio was his mistake and he'd eat the cost of it, and the fact that it had less miles was simply a bonus.

"Oh, and one more thing," Ben said. "Don't try to put it in fifth gear until after the break-in period at the five thousand mile inspection." He figured he'd drive Jim's car until she brought it in for the five thousand mile service, switch the two out then, and no one would be the wiser.

It would have worked all right except for the boyfriend. He couldn't wait to drive it, and when he couldn't get it in fifth gear, he pulled it up to the shop and asked Marty, the service manager, to take a look at it. Marty spilled the beans, and within minutes the boyfriend and the girl were in my office. I told him to calm down, that I didn't know what happened but somehow we'd make it right. Then I went out and talked to Ben. At first he was mad at Marty for not covering for him.

"What was he thinking?" he said. "It had our badge on the back. Before he said anything he should have come and talked to me."

"Don't try to push this off on Marty," I said. "He was just doing his job. This is on your head, and you're going to go in there, tell them what happened, and try to make it right."

The two of us went back in, told them what happened, and offered to put them in Jim's demo and give them a five hundred dollar service and parts credit for their trouble. As always, Ben gave them the smile and a little wink, but the boyfriend wasn't having any of it.

"We're going to sue," he said. "You guys are crooks! We want our money back and our trade-in back, or we're going to the cops."

"Hold on," I said. "Ben stepped over the line here, there's no doubt about that, and I'll deal with him later, but I found out about this when you did, and I didn't try to cover it up. I came in here and laid my cards face up on the table, and I'm now willing to do whatever it takes to make this right."

I told Ben to leave us alone, and after a few minutes the boyfriend calmed down some. I offered to order them what they wanted in next year's model at no additional cost, and I said that they could continue to drive the demo until their new one came in.

"What about the bank?" he asked. "All the paperwork is wrong."

"I'll take care of the bank and the state," I said. "Give me a chance to make this right." Eventually they agreed, and once again, I'd bailed Ben out. When I told Al, he thought it was funny, but I wasn't laughing.

Nowadays, when someone says to me, "Do you ever miss the car business?" I think about days like that and I say, "Not very much."

For a while we drove along Oceania Drive in silence as I was thinking more about what Ahbee had said. Lately, it seemed, I'd been so busy reading the Bible looking for the answers to the questions that people ask me every day that I'd stopped asking questions of my own. It had become a duty instead of a privilege, a have-to instead of a get-to, and that had to change.

Ahbee pulled off the road and parked the Volvo on the rocks overlooking the sea. "Lunchtime," he announced, grabbing the little picnic basket from the backseat. "We're going Mediterranean. Hope you don't mind."

With that, he began to unpack the basket. It was full of coarse brown bread with nuts, dried cherries, yellow raisins and cream cheese, green olives stuffed with feta cheese, two small fish that had been breaded and deep-fried, some dried dates, and a small flask of sparkling white grape juice.

As we ate, he asked me a question. "Do you remember what Joshua said when they asked him what the greatest commandment was?"

"Yes," I replied. "Love the Lord your God with all your heart, soul, and mind. And love your neighbor as yourself."

"Very good! Now, do you do this?"

"I try."

"That's your problem: you're trying too hard. Love is at its best when it's simply an expression of who you are. Josh didn't *try* to love the world, he just loved them, and that's what you have to do. You need to stop trying so hard to fix people and just love them for who they are and where they are. When they see that, when they know that you really care, then they'll be more willing to listen to what you have to say."

His words went through my heart like a knife. "That's not fair!" I protested. "Many times I have loved the unlovable for your sake. Most of the people I deal with are wrestling with demons of some kind. Their marriages are hanging on by a thread, or their addictions have got them by the throat, or their regrets are eating them up inside, and without me they'd fall off the precipices.

"And as for those who do fall," I continued, "well, it's not my fault if they don't take my advice. Besides, most of them don't really want to change. What they want is for me to baptize their stupidity. To tell them that what they're doing is all right. I'm the last stop on the bus in their minds. A hoop they have to jump through before they do what they want. That way they can tell their friends they tried. I may not be perfect, but I'm a better Christian than most people."

Who are you keeping from falling today?

"I agree." Ahbee nodded. "You're right, but most people haven't had the education, the influence, or the opportunities that you've had. There's no need for you to get defensive. Being a Christian isn't a contest where the best score wins. I know exactly what you've done. Like Moses, you've kept people from falling at times. But who are you keeping from falling today?

"Your words have been an inspiration to some, and your kindness has been a comfort to others, but there have also been those you have chosen not to love. You're a selective lover; you don't love equally, and you know it. And to be perfectly honest about it, sometimes you love sin more than you love me, and you know that too."

"Has anyone ever told you that you reading their hearts can be very unnerving?" I asked, trying to turn the conversation in a different direction.

"Yes," Ahbee said. "I've heard that many times, but we were talking about you, not me. You expect a lot from yourself, and that's good. You have high standards. My standards. No one could say that you haven't poured your heart and soul into everything you've done. I've heard your prayers for Ben, and for others, and I've watched you try your best to help him. But I'm afraid that sometimes you expect too much from the people around you."

For a moment Ahbee paused, putting his hand to his chin as if he were thinking, and then he continued. "Florence was right when she said you should never miss the chance to make someone's life better. But sometimes you do. I know you don't mean to, but you do. You can be a little intimidating. It's hard for others to stand in your shadow, and at times that's been a source of pride to you, but it breaks my heart.

"Never have I told you to work harder," Ahbee continued, "but many times I've said to love deeper. Do you have any idea what a word of encouragement from you could mean to Ben? I don't expect you to save the world, but I do expect you to save those you can, and Ben is in that camp. Like so many others, he really struggles with self-doubt and insecurity. Whether you know it or not, he looks up to you. He always has, and so you need to work at being a little more gracious.

"What I want is to be able to welcome you home someday with the words, 'Well done, good and faithful servant,' and I know that's what you want too. But I've got to tell you that the measuring stick in my kingdom is not what you have or what you've accomplished; it's who you've helped. I'm much more concerned with *people* than *performance*, and this is your chance to make a difference.

God never asked us to work harder, but he has asked us to love deeper.

"You have a lifetime of experience. Don't you think it's time you shared some of it? Come on, Scout, it's time for you to do this. I want you to share your successes, but most of all I want you to share your failures. Let Ben go to school on your mistakes. Become the coach I know you can be. Teach him; inspire him; challenge, motivate, and encourage him. Pour yourself into him. That's what brothers do, and that's what brotherly love is all about. Just as I believe in you, so too you need to believe in him. I know you can do this!"

hope

Most of the important things in the world have
been accomplished by people who have kept on
trying when there seemed to be no hope at all.

Dale Carnegie

10

On the way back, I was feeling a little sorry for myself, and a little underappreciated too.

"Ahbee," I said, "how can you be so hard on me? If I had stayed in the car business, I'd be a millionaire by now. After years of sacrifice and education, I still make less now than I used to because I believed you wanted me to help people. I am one of the few who read the story of the rich young ruler and took it to heart. Don't I get any credit for that?"

"No one is questioning your willingness to sacrifice, Scout," Ahbee said. "Or your deep desire to make a difference. That's why you're here. Because of that, I wanted to give you a chance to get out ahead on this. I'm hoping that you can share some of the things that I've shared with you, but before you challenge people to search their souls, I thought you ought to do a little soul-searching yourself."

"Maybe I'll just go up to bed early tonight," I replied.

"That's up to you," Ahbee said, "but I think maybe you'll change your mind when you see who's waiting for you back at the cottage."

Curious but cautious, I kept my thoughts to myself, and the rest of the ride back was pretty quiet. The windows were down, and I could hear the whining, rhythmic sound of the tires against the pavement. I laid my head against the side window, and my thoughts and my eyes grew heavy.

I must have fallen asleep because I woke up with a start as the tires on the Volvo hit the gravel driveway of the cottage. There, parked in front of the garage door, was a fire engine–red '53 Buick Roadmaster convertible. The only person I knew who ever drove a car like that was my uncle Herb.

Before we challenge others to search their souls, we should do a little soul-searching ourselves.

"Herby!" I shouted as I jumped out of the Volvo. He came around the corner from the front of the house and gave me his usual greeting.

"Hi, how-are-you, hi, how-are-you?" he asked, in a singsong sort of a way that mimicked the Indian drums of an old western movie.

Uncle Herb was wearing tattered leather loafers, white tube socks, seersucker Bermuda shorts, a navy blue Hope College sweatshirt, and his signature yellow vest. Before he went into the Marines, Herb had been a tailback at Hope College. Twenty years later, I followed him there.

There was a thing that my mother called the Herb-Sky-Dave syndrome because Herby, my cousin Dave, and I all had to learn things the hard way. Too often we masked our insecurities with bravado, and in our younger days, we all had a reputation for being hot-headed and quick to fight. They were both tougher than I was, but what I lacked in toughness I made up for in bullheaded stupidity, which was sometimes mistaken for bravery. Mercifully, we all outgrew most of that and became lovers instead of fighters.

I stuck my hand out to greet him, but Herby was a hugger. He believed that the world would be a better place if people hugged more often. He grabbed me, picked me off the ground, and said, "Hope you're hungry, Tiger." I suddenly realized I was starving.

Uncle Herb was my dad's younger brother and had been his closest friend. Ten years separated them, but they'd had one heart. They fished together, hunted together, and vacationed together, and most of the time, they let me tag along.

Herb and Gerry were the cool aunt and uncle everyone wished they had. I remember when I was four years old and they pulled up in front of our house on Hazan Street in that red Buick, and the next thing I knew, I was sitting on Aunt Gerry's lap and we were going for a ride.

When Uncle Herb honked the horn, it went *Ahuuuuga! Ahuuuuga!* That started my lifelong love affair with cars. Dad always drove station wagons—sturdy, practical, dependable, roomy, and boring—but Herby thought cars ought to be fun, and I agreed.

The world would be a better place if people hugged more often.

Uncle Herb was named after Grandpa, but he was given the letter P as a middle initial to avoid mail mix-ups. Nobody knew for sure what the P stood for, but Grandma used to joke that it meant, "Please, God, don't let him be anything like his father." Thankfully, he wasn't.

Like Grandma, Herby knew how to laugh and he knew how to love. Later in life, when Gerry had Alzheimer's, it robbed her of who she was little by little, but Herb never forgot who she was, and he never stopped loving her. She was the love of his life. The two of them fit together like cherry pie and ice cream. I can't think of one without thinking of the other.

I don't remember it, but I was the ring bearer at their wedding the same year that I rode in that Buick. Looking through their wedding pictures, I thought Gerry was the most beautiful woman I'd ever seen. I think Herb thought so too, and from what I could tell, his feelings never changed.

———

"Sky's here!" Herb hollered as we walked out in front of the cottage. Gerry rose from the lawn chair she was sitting in. She looked as young as she did in their wedding pictures, with long, flowing, rusty brown hair; high cheekbones covered in freckles; and a smile that would melt your heart. She was wearing red shorts, a white sleeveless blouse with a blue rope and anchor around the collar, a big floppy straw hat, and a pair of Foster Grant sunglasses.

Gerry was a hugger too, and as she put her arms around me, I noticed that she smelled like flowers and baby oil. Then she laughed for no particular reason. She had a great laugh, and even when everything else was taken from her, the laugh never left her.

On the table in the screened-in porch was potato salad, ice-cold lemonade, and sliced homegrown tomatoes. Herb was butter-basting chicken pieces on the charcoal grill outside. He always slow-cooked it over low coals, and then right before it was done, he'd switch from basting with butter to barbeque sauce.

Even when everything else is taken from us, we can still laugh.

The sauce was a recipe Carol and I received from the chef at a restaurant we frequented when we were dating and she has tweaked over the years. She freely passed it out to everyone, and my family has put it on everything. It's a thick, sweet, tomato-based sauce, and there was a mason jar full of it sitting on a tray next to the grill. Herby painted it on each piece with a brush, and as soon as he got them all basted on one side, he'd turn them over and do the same on the other side. As the brown sugar in the sauce began to caramelize, the chicken turned golden brown and crispy.

Alongside the chicken Herb was grilling salmon. He'd made a boat of aluminum foil, placed the salmon filet skin-side down, and then placed six pats of butter on top. Then he poured a half a bottle of French dressing over the fish, liberally loaded it with parmesan cheese, and sprinkled it with salt, pepper, and dill.

"It's all about the timing," Herby said as he stuck a meat thermometer into one of the chicken breasts, and after a minute or two, he announced it was time to eat. He plated up the chicken and the fish, brought them inside, and then got a little choked up as he said grace.

After supper we moved to the living room and talked mostly about the people we loved.

"I miss your dad," he said.

"He misses you too," I replied. "More than you know."

"And my boys too," Herby added.

"They're all doing fine," I said. "Both of them are kind of growing into your shoes, Herb. Dave's more like you every day, and you'd be so proud of Steve. Since he quit drinking, he's become the man you always knew he could be. Like you, his heart is tender toward anyone in need."

"I always knew he could stop drinking," Herb said. "I couldn't, but I knew he could."

He got a little emotional, and Gerry moved closer to him and put her arm around his neck. We sat in front of the fireplace, roasted a couple of marshmallows, and talked about what was and what will be as it slowly became dark. Time has a way of getting away from you sometimes, and this was one of those times.

Finally he got around to asking about Ben. "How's your little brother doing?" he asked.

"To be honest, I'm a little worried about him," I said. "He's never gotten over what happened up at the lake. Money's a problem, Mary Alice is a problem, and spiritually I don't know where he's at."

"Maybe you know more than you're telling," Herb said.

"What do you mean by that?" I asked.

"Two weeks ago you saw him come forward crying like a baby when Pastor Bill asked if anyone wanted to come up and leave their past on the altar."

"I saw him," I said. "I'm just not sure I believe him."

"Oh, so now you are the judge of who's sincere and who's not?"

"No, I'm not saying that. It's just I know some things, that's all."

"You know some things, but you don't know everything. Besides, right now he's been trying to make it right, and maybe he will and maybe he won't, but you've got to give him time. You of all people can't give up on him. Hope is all he has, and he's hanging on to that by a thread. Right now he needs you to believe in him more than anything else.

"Listen," he continued, "he comes from a long line of prodigals. Some of us are slow learners. We have to learn everything the hard way, and we take our own sweet time doing it. Give him time, Sky, give him a little more time." Then he got up and started to walk toward the door.

Where there is no hope, there is no life.

"Come on, Tons-of-Fun," Herb said to Gerry. "We've got a little bit of a ride, and Ernie will be by pretty early tomorrow morning."

Ernie was my great-uncle on Grandma's side, and when Dad and Herb were young, Ernie always took them hunting, and they returned the favor later in life.

"What are you guys doing?" I asked.

"Oh, Ernie wants to go do a little bass fishing up at Promise Point," Herb said.

As we walked outside, I hugged Gerry good-bye and opened the Buick's side door for her. Then I went around to Herb's side. "There's something I need to tell you," he said to me. "Where there is no hope there is no life. You have to *hold on to hope even when things look hopeless.*"

"In my heart I know that's true," I said, "but sometimes I feel like the hope has dried up inside of me."

"That's why I'm here. I know what you're going through. I've been right where Ben is too. Some days, faith comes easy, it's smooth as butter, but sometimes, doubt smothers our faith like a wet blanket. On those days you want to believe, you kind of believe, you wish you would fully believe, but doubt has got you by the throat. Am I right?"

"You must have been reading my mail," I said.

"I haven't, but God has," he said. "And that's why I'm here. Just because you got a hot-shot counseling degree doesn't mean you're not human. You're no different than the rest of us. We hope and we fear. We pray with confidence and we worry. We believe, and God help us, we doubt.

"In the book of Jude, the author says to 'be merciful to those who doubt.' Who do you think he's talking about? Everybody has doubts. No one is immune. That's just the way it is. And if you try to deny it, if you swallow your doubts, if you keep putting a Band-Aid on your broken faith, it'll fester. You've got to deal with it. You've got to talk about it. You've got to get it out in the open. And that's where prayer comes in," Herby explained.

"Listen," I responded, "I've always prayed. Sometimes out of gratitude, sometimes out of fear, and often out of habit, but lately I've been wondering if it makes any difference. I guess I've just seen too many unanswered prayers."

"There's no such thing as an unanswered prayer," Herb said. "Sometimes the answer is 'No,' and sometimes it's 'Not now,' but it's never *not* answered. Usually what happens is that we don't like or don't understand the answers we get, and so we think that Ahbee has failed the test, but it's really just the opposite."

"I'm not sure I get what you mean by that."

"Well, don't you put Ahbee to the test every time you pray? If he answers, if you get what you want, he passes, but if he doesn't, then you start to question him. Am I right?"

"Well, I guess that's the way it works sometimes," I answered.

"So like I said, when you pray, you're really putting God to the test. But what if it is the other way around? What if you are the one being tested?"

"I guess I've never thought about it that way before," I said. "Besides, the whole idea that God tests people never made much sense to me. For example, why would a loving God tell Abraham to sacrifice his son by burning him on an altar? It always seemed like a barbaric exercise to me. What was the point of that? If

God knows everything, he already knew what Abraham would do before he asked."

"God knew, but Abraham didn't," Herby explained. "The point was not that God would learn whether Abraham was committed to him; the point was that Abraham would learn how committed he was to God. He needed to know the depth of his own faith. And like with Abraham, sometimes prayer simply reminds us who's in charge of the universe. Acknowledging that God is still God helps us stretch our faith around the things we don't understand. Prayer changes things, and when it doesn't change our circumstances, it changes our heart. You have to believe that! Don't give up, don't quit, keep believing in yourself, and keep believing in God.

"Ultimately, the victory isn't up to you. God has a plan, and he's working his will in the world, even when we don't see it. Sometimes the flames of hope flicker in the winds of life, and the darkness looks like it's going to have its way with the world—but it won't. So when things start to look bleak, you need to stand a little taller, a little stronger, and a little braver than everyone else. People look to you for encouragement, so you need to take the lead, to be the example, to set the table for hope.

"Trust me, one day you'll see it all more clearly. Here there's no more pain, no more crying, no more doubt, and no more dying. Everything makes sense. All the pieces fit together. But until you get here, you need to be a champion for hope."

Herby ended with, "Tell my boys what I said, and tell them that I love them."

He was getting choked up, and so was I, but I could tell that they were tears of confidence and optimism.

"When did you get to be such an expert on hope?" I asked.

Herby responded, "A few months before the cancer finally had its way with me, I was trying to make sense of it all. 'Where are you in all this, God?' I asked. 'Why did this have to happen to me, why did Gerry get Alzheimer's, and who's going to take care of her when I'm gone?' I was talking to Ahbee about it, and I wasn't pulling any punches.

"Then suddenly I heard a voice say to me, 'Herby, my son, you're not God, I am. You don't have to worry about the things you can't control. That's my job. Have I ever failed you before? So what makes you think I will fail you now? I am the hope of the world, and I am your hope too.'

"I realized in that moment that although I could not see him, God saw me, and he had things well in hand. I guess when there seems to be no hope, you suddenly realize that God is our only hope."

As they drove away, Gerry waved and I heard one last *Ahuuuuga!* as the Buick disappeared into the trees.

limitations

I seldom think about my limitations and they
never make me sad. Perhaps there's a touch of
yearning at times, but it's vague, like a breeze
among the flowers.

Helen Keller

11

Ahbee was cordial but quiet at breakfast. "Have you thought much about what we talked about yesterday?" he asked.

"Not as much as I need to," I admitted.

"Well then, maybe today would be a good day to just sit and think things through."

I sensed that our conversation had ended, so after a breakfast of French toast and smokey links and a little conversation with Michael, I spent the day sitting on the beach, sailing the Hobie Cat buoyed out front, and thinking about what Herby and Ahbee had said. There were things I needed to change, I knew that. I needed to be more confident, more hopeful, more of a tower of strength for those who stumble, and I needed to be less concerned about performance and more concerned about people. The question was, how?

Up until that point in my life, my formula for living had come off a Mercedes-Benz brochure I'd seen in the seventies. "The best or nothing," it read, and I liked it. It was very German, very concise, very goal-oriented, and it gave me a target to aim for. Like they say, "They give silver medals to first losers," and I wanted to win. It's funny how your attitude can affect everything about the way you live.

For too long I'd been looking at life as though it were a competition. When I was a boy, my dad gave me a handwritten note. It was printed in the clean, crisp, block capital letters that reflected his trade as a tool and die maker. It said, "Work as though everything depends on you, and pray as though everything depends on God." I had always tipped the teeter-totter toward the work side. But now I was starting to believe that I had it backwards: that if life was a competition, then the goal was not so much to finish *first* as it was to finish *well*.

Work as though everything depends on you. Pray as though everything depends on God.

It was time I came to grips with the fact that I'm not a kid anymore. In fact, I'm on the downward slide. I can't see the finish line, but I know I'm probably closer to it than the starting blocks. If adjustments were going to be made in my life, now was the time. I set the jib on the Hobie and headed for the buoy.

The sun hung low in the sky as I buoyed the sailboat and swam back to shore. I made my way up the front steps of the cottage, and that's when I saw it—a rusted lime-green Chevy Vega was parked in the driveway. The rear bumper was crumpled and the right taillight was broken. Clearly the car had seen better days, but I recognized it immediately. It belonged to DL, my uncle David Lee. Actually, it was titled in my name, but it was DL's nonetheless.

———

DL was my mother's youngest brother. He was a trailer born to Jack and Esther late in life, almost twenty years after Mom and Don. Everyone always knew that DL was different, but nobody wanted to admit it, much less talk about it. So for the first fifty years of his life, DL went without being diagnosed as autistic.

As we grew up, my siblings and I heard little bits and pieces whispered from time to time by my parents in another room, but no one ever said much in front of us. When they did, it was basically about how smart DL was as a toddler until he fell out of that swing and hit his head. Grandma Jacobs insisted that he was never right after that. The rest of us never really bought into all that, but we kept our opinions to ourselves around her.

After Grandpa Jack died, Uncle Don and my dad were able to get DL a driver's license so he could cart Grandma around, but he never should have been on the road. The man drove by feel. He'd pull up to something ever so slowly until he felt a thump. The bumpers on every vehicle DL owned would be bent up within a month. He banged into street signs, fire hydrants, brick walls, light poles in parking lots, and of course, other cars.

The goal of life is not to finish first but to finish well.

If the autism wasn't bad enough, DL started drinking after Grandma died. Every week my mom would give him money for food, which he would spend on beer and cigarettes, and before long he was hooked.

Once when I was a kid, the phone rang at two thirty in the morning. A few minutes later my dad stood in my doorway and said, "Get dressed. It's time you saw this."

We drove over to Grandma's house. DL was sitting in his boxers leaning back in Grandpa's recliner, wide-eyed and whimpering. "Do you see them?" he shouted, pointing into the shadows of the dining room.

"See what?" Dad asked.

"The demons! They're coming for me!"

Unfortunately, they already had him. Darkness has a way of dredging up old doubts and fears, and DL was totally out of touch with reality. He wildly shadowboxed his demons and yelled, "Look out! Look out!" Then he turned his rage on Dad and screamed, "You're with them!"

Dad tried to assure DL that he wasn't with them, but by this time DL was seeing demons everywhere. He started throwing empty beer bottles, smashing them against the wall, and eventually one crashed through the living room window. Dodging bottles, Dad finally tackled him and held him to the ground.

"Give me your belt," he said, in a voice I remember thinking was way too calm. I gave Dad my belt, and he strapped DL's arms behind his back.

By this time, ol' DL was kicking and screaming and yelling, "Don't let them take me, Jesus! I'll be good, I promise, I don't want to go back to hell!"

Darkness has a way of dredging up old doubts and fears.

From what I could see, DL was already in hell, at least in his mind, and seeing him like that scared me.

"It's just the alcohol talking," Dad explained. "He doesn't mean it, and he can't help it. He's out of his head right now. Tomorrow he'll sober up, and he'll be his normal self."

At some point DL passed out, and we unceremoniously carried him out to the car. We buckled him in the backseat of the Vista Cruiser and took him down to the Salvation Army Rehabilitation Center's drunk tank. There DL got loved sober. He lived at the Salvation Army for a couple years under the watchful eye of his guardian angel, a man by the name of Major Metts.

Dad had to sell Grandma's house to pay for DL's treatment, and when he was released, we moved him to a room at the Lighthouse Mission. There DL played piano for their meetings, and he also guarded the shower room door whenever the women went inside to make sure that no unsavory characters went in after them.

There was a lot about life that DL didn't understand. Life had treated him unfairly. He was autistic and an alcoholic. When God was passing out talents, DL only got two. First, he had a thing for numbers, particularly days and dates (if you've seen the movie *Rain Man*, you know what I'm talking about). If you told DL your birthday, he could tell you what day of the week you were born.

"November eleven, nineteen-eighty—one, one, one, one, eight, zero. That was a Tuesday, yes, a Tuesday, I'm sure of it." Or suppose you wanted to know the circumference of, say, Mars or Pluto, or its distance from the sun—well then, DL was your man.

But his other talent, his real talent, was music. The autism giveth and the autism taketh away, and what it gave DL was the piano. If he heard a song once, he could play it. And he'd play it over and over again. Since playing piano was his one and only usable talent, he used it whenever he could.

Life isn't always fair, but God is always good, and he even used DL in his broken condition. He played twice a week at the county jail, every Wednesday at the Christian Businessmen's Luncheon, every other Sunday night at Grand Avenue Christian Reformed Church, and every Saturday night for the re-commitment service at the Lighthouse Mission where he lived.

Life isn't always fair, but God is always good.

It sounds real nice, and it was, but the problem was that DL was short on social graces. He was rough and gruff and not easy to be around. Because of that, he didn't have many friends. My sister, brother, and I were as close to him as anyone, but honestly, it was a duty for me. It was a promise I'd made to my mother to look after her little brother. So when he needed Aqua Velva, or new socks, or another electric razor, I'd get it for him. My sister was more of a reflection of my mother, and so when she'd stop by, she'd bring cookies and conversation. As for Ben, he had the patience of Job. He never seemed to mind DL's peculiar ways, and sometimes he'd let him wash cars at the lot for a little extra spending money.

As a family, we always had what my kids called "DL's Christmas." We'd go over to my mom and dad's a couple nights after Christmas Day, and we'd all get him something. Mostly it was clothes, but we'd get him cookies, and candy, and passes to the movies too. We'd sit around and watch him open his presents, and then we'd eat dinner. DL would always tell us that this was his third or fourth Christmas dinner. He had one at the mission, another one at the jail, and sometimes he'd get invited to somebody's house who used to live at the mission.

Every Christmas, my daughter Kate would get him to tell the shoe polish story. "Once I knew a man," he'd start, "who was so addicted to the liquor that when he couldn't get any, he'd pour shoe polish through a loaf of bread, and then he'd drink it. I know you don't believe me," he'd say, "but it's true." And then he'd get all misty. We knew that someone was him, but we acted like we didn't know. The stories that affect us most are the ones that are about us, and that's why we keep coming back to the stories of the Bible. Christmas is a story of redemption, and so after DL would tell his redemption story, we'd all say "Merry Christmas" and go home. The rest of us would go home to our nice houses in the suburbs, but DL would go to his room at the Lighthouse Mission.

The stories that affect us most are the ones that are about us.

I was with him the night he died. By then he was living at the Good Shepherd home, and the nurse there called to tell me that his time was short. I went by one last time to say good-bye and to read to him from Luke's gospel. It was his favorite, and hearing it soothed his soul. He lay quietly with his eyes closed while I read, and his breathing was so shallow that I thought maybe he'd already passed.

"You know God loves you, don't you, DL?" I asked.

"I know. But don't stop. Keep reading. I like to hear it."

I did as he asked, and a few minutes later, very faintly he whispered, "Do you hear it? Do you hear the music?" I didn't but said I did, and he died a few minutes later. I have no doubt that when DL knocked on the door of heaven, he heard the Master say, "Well done, thou good and faithful servant."

184

That was three years ago now, and here he was sitting on the steps of the back porch. As I walked up, DL greeted me with the line he always used whenever he'd call my house in need of something. "IS SKY THERE?" he would say, loud and gruff and teetering on the edge of anger. But then he smiled. "Hello, little brother," he said in a gentle voice that neither I nor anyone else had often heard him use before. It was DL, but it wasn't. He looked different. First off, he had curly blond hair. I'd seen him with that hair in old pictures, but for as long as I could remember, he was as bald as an eagle.

Second, he didn't have glasses. DL always wore thick Coke-bottle glasses that were often taped together in some way because he'd broken them. If he broke a lot of cars, he broke even more pairs of glasses, and between visits to the eye doctor, he would tape the frames together with white athletic tape.

Third, he seemed taller and certainly thinner. Once, when my wife wanted to buy him some new pants, she asked him what size he was. DL said that he was a perfect 40-30. A 40-inch waist, 30-inch inseam. My girls said he looked like a Weeble, the little round toy dolls that bounced back up when you knocked them over.

<hr />

One year when I was in junior high, my parents rented a cottage up at Stony Lake, and because they knew that if they didn't take DL on their vacation, he wouldn't get a vacation, they invited him along. My siblings and I were mortified at this thought, but when Dad said, "Family is family," we knew it was final.

Mostly DL stayed by the cottage, but one afternoon while I was talking to my friends down at the public beach, he came walking down the road. "Who's that weirdo with his pants pulled up to his armpits?" someone asked.

I did my best to pretend I didn't know him until he walked up and said, "Hi, Sky."

At times I was embarrassed to be his nephew, but he was always proud to be my uncle. Whenever I'd visit him at the mission, he'd always tell everyone that I had to call him uncle. Then he'd look at them as if to say, "That's right, I'm his uncle."

No matter what you do, God will never pretend that he doesn't know you.

In later years, DL would tell anyone who'd listen that I was a major, the rank he thought I'd earned in the Salvation Army. In his mind, anybody who'd gone to graduate school automatically got commissioned as an officer like the preacher at the rehabilitation center. I'd try to correct him, but he didn't listen. It annoyed me. "I'm not in the Salvation Army, DL," I'd say. "I'm a psychologist." But he kept saying it.

Then one day when we were out getting him a haircut, he told me that he called me Major because I reminded him of Major Metts. Metts was his hero. He was one step below God. I realized then that in DL's mind, I was his protector, the one who watched out for him. So I stopped correcting him.

"What's for dinner?" DL asked, bringing me back to the moment.

"Why are you asking me?" I replied. "I thought you'd be making me dinner like everyone else."

"Not this time, Major," he said. "You're the chef tonight."

Actually, the idea of making dinner sounded good to me. At first I thought I'd make bread and milk. It was a Jacobs thing. You fried up pork fat in a pan, added whole milk, salt, and pepper, and after it thickened, you would dunk stale bread in it. I know—it sounds awful. But trust me, if you were raised on it, it was a little taste of heaven.

"What are you hungry for?" I asked.

"Something I used to have at the mission. Surprise me. You know what I like."

That made it easy because there wasn't much DL didn't like. But the more I thought about it, the more I leaned toward chicken soup. The mission made great chicken soup "like Ma used to make," DL would say.

Sometimes when DL said "Ma," he meant Grandma Jacobs, and sometimes he meant my mother. Fortunately for me, they used the same recipe. It started with a roasting chicken. The trick was to slow cook it in a stockpot on top of the stove for hours. Then when it was falling off the bones, you took it out of the pan and pulled the meat off the bone. Half of it would be reserved for sandwiches or something, and the other half went back in the pot with the broth. Then you'd add vegetables, seasoning, and rice. The problem was, it took all day, and I didn't have that kind of time.

But when I walked into the kitchen my time concerns evaporated. Ahbee had already done the grocery shopping for me. A stockpot was already simmering on the stove.

I looked under the lid and found a roasting chicken falling off the bone. Chicken soup is a combination of what the recipe calls for and what's in the house, so as always, I improvised a little. Along with the other ingredients, I added long grain wild rice, mushrooms, and a small bowl of corn that had just been cut off the cob. Under a towel on the table I found a loaf pan with dense, dark, grainy bread dough of some kind rising inside.

God knows our thoughts before we do.

It was getting dark by the time we sat down to dinner. We pulled up a couple of chairs at the little table in the kitchen, and I ladled the soup into some large bowls that I found in the cupboard. DL sliced the bread and I buttered a piece for each of us. Then he prayed in a soft, gentle voice, "My Father, you welcome us to your table with grace, love, and forgiveness. Thank you for this meal and for this time we have together. Amen."

We sat at the table and talked well into the night about people from the past, and finally DL said, "I've got to get going, little brother. I only have one headlight, and I never did like driving after dark."

My mind went back to a night years before when we'd all been at my mom's for DL's Christmas. It was a cold December night, and the roads were dusted with freshly fallen snow. DL had left about five minutes before us, but within a couple miles we caught up to him. He was hunched over the steering wheel, creeping along in the right lane as if the road were covered in ice.

God has a special place in his heart for lost sheep.

DL had run into a fire hydrant a few weeks before, and his right front headlight tilted up at a thirty-degree angle. The light reflected off the falling snow, and Carol said that it looked like he was shining for angels. As we passed, he was talking to himself and waving his arms wildly. He was on his way back to the Lighthouse Mission, and I was struck by the irony of it all. One headlight pointed the way down the road to the mission, and the other pointed the way to heaven; either way, somehow he'd find his way home, because God has a special place in his heart for lost sheep. That night, to our surprise, this one made his way back to the mission.

As I walked him out to the car, I must have had a pained look on my face.

"What's wrong?" DL asked.

"I guess I never thought that anyone would drive a Vega in heaven," I explained. "I feel bad, because it's such a bucket of bolts. You shouldn't have to drive that!"

"I could drive any car I want," DL replied, "but material things don't really matter much here. What matters here is people, and every time I get in this car, I think of you and Ben. You bought it and he kept it running. Anytime anything would break, I'd bring it by the lot and he'd always help me out. And when I'd leave it would always be with a full tank of gas and a twenty sticking out of the glove box. You gave me whatever I needed; he gave me my dignity. Besides, I'm driving this car for your sake, not mine. It's what I have for you: *we were put on earth to serve, not to be served.*"

DL explained. "Remember what Josh said: 'What you've done to the least of these my brothers, you've done to me.' If you divide the world into two groups of people and you called one the most and one the least, you'd be numbered among the former and I'd be in the latter. There's a gap between your group and mine. That's not your fault, and it's not my fault either. It just is. There's an inequity to life. It isn't always fair. As my namesake once wrote, 'Sometimes fools ride horseback and kings and princes go barefoot.' There will come a day when that will no longer be true, but it's true enough today on earth, and no one can deny it.

We were put on this earth to serve, not to be served.

"What I'm trying to say," DL continued, "is that Ahbee doesn't expect you to correct every wrong or confront every evil, but he does expect you to correct and confront some, at least the ones he puts in your path, and you did that for me. There is no question that you were my lifeline. When I had no place else to turn, I could always turn to you. Those little acts of service from you and Sharon and Ben kept my head above water. You were your brother's keeper, or in this case, you were your uncle's keeper, and I'm eternally grateful for that.

"But I have a question for you: Who took my place? Who are you keeping now? Who needs you the way I needed you? Like I said, there's a gap between the most and the least, and what you have to ask yourself is, 'Am I filling the gap?'"

His question hung in the night air as he hugged me good-bye and drove away. I walked back inside and found Ahbee and Michael sitting at the kitchen table.

"Are you okay?" Michael asked. "You look like a man with a lot of questions."

"There's just so much I don't understand," I said, pulling a chair up to the table.

"For all your understanding," Ahbee said, "there is much you will never understand. Mystery is part of life; it's in your DNA; it's part of being human. I did not force you out into the world. There was a time when humanity knew only good, but then Adam chose to add the knowledge of evil to the human storehouse of wisdom, and it's been confusing for all of you ever since."

Ahbee paused for a moment so my thoughts could catch up with his, and my mind went back to Mrs. Johnson's Sunday school class. There on the flannelgraph a naked Adam and Eve stood behind strategically placed fig leaves and were about to bite into an apple. I remember as a young boy wanting to yell, "Don't do it!" but it was too late. Mrs. Johnson then put up a picture of Adam's face. He looked guilty as sin, and he had apple juice running down his chin. I looked up at Ahbee as if to say, "I'm with you," and he continued to explain.

God wants to share so much with us, if only we'd listen.

"In the beginning Rae, Joshua, and I wanted to share everything *except evil* with you all. Other than that there was no limit to the potential of your knowledge. But with evil came limitation. Restrictions were put in place, certain things were locked in a vault called Eden, and Michael has stood guard at the gate ever since.

"Have you ever seen someone put a drop of India ink into a pitcher of water? Immediately it pollutes and permeates every drop. Evil is like that. In an instant it swallowed knowledge in a murky cloud of uncertainty. But that does not mean that there will not be learning. Humans are always learning.

"I want to share so much with you, if only you'd take the time to listen. Things that will eliminate disease, fight poverty, and help you stand up to evil. But knowledge, in and of itself, is neutral. It can be used for good or for evil. Only the heart of the person who holds an idea can control that. My hands are tied. It's part of the promise I made a long time ago in Eden. Of all the gifts

I've given you, the most precious is the freedom to choose, and choose you must."

My mind was reeling with it all. I was on information overload, so finally I said, "Right now, I choose to go to bed."

"Sleep well," said Ahbee. "Tomorrow we'll talk more, but remember: each day life is full of choices. Do I have jelly on my toast or peanut butter? Do I go to work or stay home with my sick daughter? Every choice is fraught with consequences. The mystery unfolds around you like the flowers in a spring field.

"I am forever revealing mystery, but not all mysteries. The secrets of life, death, love, and the meaning of it all must be pursued like a lover. Mathematics, science, and technology are tools, but in and of themselves they will always fall short. Without a spiritual compass to guide you, you'll always be groping in the darkness. That's what the Bible is for—a compass for the course of life."

evil

When evil men plot, good men must plan.
When evil men burn and bomb, good men
must build and bind.

Martin Luther King Jr.

12

When I came downstairs the next morning, Josh and Michael were sitting at the dining room table drinking mugs of strong, black coffee.

Knowing I'm not a coffee drinker, Josh said, "Sit down, Scout. I'll get you a Coke."

I watched as he did, and once again I was caught off guard by his willingness to serve.

Our conversation was light, mostly about the beauty of the day, and I waited for one of them to invite me to go with them. But an invitation never came.

I could smell biscuits baking, and Josh got up every once in a while and tended to something frying in the kitchen. "What's for breakfast?" I asked.

"Oh, Josh set the menu this morning," said Michael. "It may be foreign to your palate at first, but don't knock it till you've tried it!"

A wide-mouthed jar of yogurt had already been set on the table, and next to it was a small ceramic bowl of granola and another with fresh blackberries.

"You're always safe with the yogurt," Michael said. "And the biscuits are warm and wonderful. Ahbee got up early and baked them before he left." Just at that moment, Josh came in with a platter of biscuits the size of baseballs and a mess of golden brown fish filets that he had hand-battered and then panfried.

"Buttermilk bluegills," said Josh. "They're my favorite."

"What?" I asked, perplexed.

"Oh, he's just pulling your leg," Michael explained. "As a boy, Josh would often have fish and flatbread for breakfast. It was that or goat cheese, sliced tomatoes, and green olives. So sometimes we have breakfast with a Mediterranean flair. He dips the bluegills in buttermilk and then breads them in buckwheat pancake flour. Josh likes them best with goat cheese and sliced green olives, but I'd recommend the biscuits and honey instead."

I'm not a big fan of seafood, but Josh's bluegills were remarkably good. Feeling adventurous, I tried the goat cheese and green olives with a slice of tomato on my biscuit, but I was with Michael: I preferred the honey.

I cleared the dishes after breakfast and offered to clean up. "I'd appreciate that," Josh said. "Michael and I have some errands to run."

Josh poured himself another cup of coffee, and the two of them went out the back door, got in Josh's truck, and drove away.

Uncertain of what waited for me, I washed the breakfast dishes, then went out on the front porch. The sun was just coming up, and the orange and yellow streaks of color danced across the ripples of the lake. The stillness of the morning was striking. Simon and Garfunkel were right: there's something about the sound of silence. It's peaceful.

I looked back through the door and stared at the words that were carved in the mantel of the fireplace. "Peace I leave with you. My peace I give to you." I realized that I'd let my life get so overscheduled that I hadn't made time for God. I decided that was going to change, and peace settled over me like a warm blanket. I hadn't felt this peaceful in a long, long time. There was no rush here, no schedules or deadlines, no sense of urgency.

Perhaps that's what's the matter with most of us, I thought. *We're in such a hurry to get where we're going that we don't take the time to appreciate where we are.*

Suddenly I had a moment of clarity. It dawned on me that if we don't know where we are, we can't know where we're going. It's like when you go to the mall looking for a particular store and you come across one of those kiosks with a map. They list all the stores, and they have a big red arrow that says, "You are here." Otherwise you wouldn't know if you should go left or right or turn around. And life is like that too. A lot of people are on the wrong road, they're headed in the wrong direction, but instead of turning around or stopping to ask for directions, they just try to run faster and faster. I know because I was right there with them. But somehow being here had helped me to slow down, to get my bearings, and to redirect my life toward the things that really matter.

Life can get so overscheduled that we don't make time for God.

The morning spilled into afternoon, and I was so engrossed in thought that I failed to notice a car quietly pull up the driveway—a silver Mercedes SLC with blue leather interior. The wire wheels and wide tires were aftermarket, but everything else was stock. It was a 4.5 liter, dual overhead cam, ram air V8, stealthy quiet at idle but a rumbler when you put your foot into it.

"Hey, pard!" a familiar voice called out.

"Al!" I exclaimed. "Al, it's so good to see you!"

Al Roth had been my boss and then my business partner when I was in the automobile business. I started working for him at Precision Cars while I was in college, and he said I was a natural. In a matter of months I was his top salesman, and I loved it. Al had a bell on his office wall, and whenever anyone sold a car, they got to ring it. Soon I was ringing the bell more than anyone. If it was the first sale of the day, Al would say, "Every time the bell rings, an angel gets his wings," and then he'd whip out his wallet and give you a twenty dollar bill as a bonus.

Everybody knew that line from an old Christmas movie, but Al had adapted it. He never got tired of saying it, and I never got tired of hearing it, because we both knew it was the sound of money. Later that year, when I won Volvo's national sales award, he was the one who talked me into taking a job with their district office in Chicago.

A true friend never holds you back.

In his younger days, Al had followed a similar path, taking a job with Mercedes-Benz and working his way up to vice president of their American operation before buying the dealership.

"This is a real opportunity for you," he said. "I'm going to miss you, but you can't pass this up." A true friend never holds you back, so Al sent me packing.

It was on his advice that I took that job, and it was on his advice that I left it to buy the local Volkswagen dealership with him. Who your friends are often determines what you do, and Al was a true friend. He was the major stockholder and the money, but he would say that I was the energy. In those days I ran full tilt, wide-open, all day long. It was a good partnership, better than most. He let me run things pretty much on my own, and being young and cocky, I made more than a few mistakes. But I made him a lot of money too, so he was always gracious and always coaching me.

When Al's wife, Jane, learned she had cancer, we merged his Mercedes and Volvo dealership into our Volkswagen dealership so I could keep an eye on business and he could keep an eye on Jane and the kids. We kept the name Precision Cars, and for the next five years we were partners.

Then, a few months after Jane died, Al came to the office and said, "It's just not any fun for me anymore, Sky. I always said when it stops being fun, I'll stop doing this, and now's as good a time as any. I want to sell out, and if you want to buy it, I'll cosign your loan at the bank."

For a while I tried to talk him out of it, but his mind was made up. That night I went home and announced to Carol that we were going to be rich. To my surprise, she was less enthusiastic than I thought she'd be.

"I thought eventually Al was going to come back to work and you wouldn't have to work so many hours anymore," Carol said.

Then Carol asked me the question that changed our lives forever. "Come here," she said, walking down the hall to our daughter Kate's room. "When's the last time you held her in your arms during the day, other than on a Sunday?"

Who your friends are often determines what you do.

"I don't know," I admitted. "It's been a while, I guess."

Kate was just over a year old, and Carol was pregnant with Kelly, and I don't know if it was God or the hormones talking, but her question stopped me cold. "Don't you think we ought to at least pray about it?" she asked.

"Sure," I replied. "We can pray, but I can't think of one good reason that God wouldn't want us to do this. Besides, my brother Ben, your brother Gary, and my cousin Dave all work for us. What's going to happen to them if we leave?"

"They'll be okay," Carol said. "Gary's the sales manager and Ben's the top salesman. Anyone who buys that place would be a fool to let them go. And Dave's an A mechanic. He can get a job anywhere he wants. You opened the door for them, but they walked through it. Each of them has earned everything they've got."

Inside, I knew she was right. Gary was the new car sales manager not because he was my brother-in-law but because he was good at it. He was detail oriented with a head for business, and he was great with people. The employees and the customers all liked him and respected him. If something came up and I wasn't there, they'd ask Gary.

As for Ben, he'd found a home in the car business. He knew cars, he knew people, and he was smooth as whipped cream. If he wasn't selling cars for me, he'd be selling cars somewhere.

Dave was young. I hired him right out of high school, but he was as good a wrench as we had. The kid had a future in the car business with me or without me, and that was simply a fact. Carol was right: they'd all be fine. I wasn't thinking about them as much as the money and the perks.

"I don't know if this is the way I want to live the rest of my life," Carol said.

"I don't know what to say to that, Carol," I said. "I think the way we're living is just fine." At the time we were living in a house we designed and built in the woods on a hill overlooking the Thornapple River. Carol was driving a Porsche convertible. We were living the dream—at least, we were living *my* dream. It was a life of big cigars and motor cars, and I thought it was about perfect, but I said okay, if she wanted me to, I'd pray about it.

The problem is that when you ask God what he really wants you to do with your life, he usually tells you, and a couple years later we were living in a small two-bedroom house in Grandville, eating government cheese, and I was going to grad school. Like my momma always said, "Be careful what you ask for—you're liable to get it." This wasn't exactly what Carol had in mind that night when she quizzed me about Kate, but over the years, we've come to believe that it was what God had in mind. Still, there are days when memories of the car business still call to me, and seeing Al brought it all back.

When you discover that everything you always wanted isn't enough, it's time to check your priorities.

Al was short—five foot six—freckled, bald, and leathery from years of smoking. When we started in business together, he was about the most honest man I knew, a real straight arrow. If he said it was so, trust me, it was so. You'd have thought he was a devout Christian, but he wasn't. He had a bad taste in his mouth for Christians, particularly my tribe of Dutch Reformers. Before I came along, he had been in business for a while with a guy who kept a big King James Bible on his desk. The problem was that he was as crooked as a stick, and eventually Al decided that "you Dutchers" must be reading a different Bible than the one his momma read to him. "God's okay with me," he'd say, "but I don't have much use for churches or preachers." If there was a Christian conspiracy, he wasn't going to be a part of it, so for a time he opted out of organized religion.

When Jane died, Al suddenly had a need for a preacher, but he didn't know where to find one. I called Howard Schipper, and he came with words and compassion that looked to Al like Jesus, and after that, little by little Al started to reconnect with God. He even went to church once in a while. But he never had much use for the institutions of religion. When he heard that I had decided to become a psychologist and go into Christian counseling, he sent away to some diploma mill for a mail-order clergy card, and he'd tease me with it. "I don't know *If you don't feel very close to God, maybe you need to ask yourself, "Who moved?"* why you're wasting your time going to school," he'd say. "For two hundred dollars I can get you hooked up in ten days. Besides, most people don't need counseling as much as they need a swift kick in the pants!"

He was just trying to get under my skin, but now that I've done this for twenty-five years, I'd say he was more right than wrong.

A couple years after Jane died, Al ended up back in the car business again. He put Ben in the building we owned on South Division, and whenever I'd see him, he'd always say, "There'll be a spot for you here whenever you come back to your senses." I didn't, but I came close a few times.

He and Ben would go to the dealer auction a couple times a week and buy late-model European stuff. They liked VWs and Audis, but once in a while they'd pick up a Volvo or a Benz. They liked to buy cars that were a few years old with high mileage so they could keep the price point down. Often they were able to buy three-year-old cars with 75 or 80 thousand miles for about half the price of a new one. Then Ben would touch up the scratches and spoon out the minor dents, and after a good cleanup they were ready to go on the lot. Ben had an eye for color too. A lot of reds and blacks and silvers, but never telephone green or Baptist-preacher blue. Their clientele was mostly yuppies and housewives, and Ben knew what they liked.

Al got back in the car business for two reasons. First he was bored, and second he knew Ben was struggling. He and the new owners of Precision didn't get along. The Barton brothers came from a strict family. They were dress right, cover down kind of businessmen who always had an eye on the bottom line, and Ben was more laid back like Al.

Al thought the car business ought to be fun, and he was forever horsing around. When we were partners he watched over the service and parts department and pretty much left the front end to me, but he always liked hanging around with the salesmen. He had an easy way about him, and they all liked and respected him. He expected a lot from people, and when he got it the man was generous to a fault. He loved to reward performance and always had a contest of some sort going on.

One month he'd decide that if parts and service out-grossed sales, the managers would each win a week at his cottage. The next month he'd do the same thing with the mechanics, and he was forever putting little cash spiffs on cars that had been on the lot too long. One night after we'd had a particularly good month, he had four-by-eight sheets of plywood put on top of the hoists, covered them with white tablecloths and candelabras, and treated all fifty-two employees and their families to a steak fry.

Three months later he bought a set of stainless steel cookware for everyone and sent a note home with it thanking the wives for letting their husbands put in a few extra hours. Like I said, he made it fun.

One day Al came in with one of those "take a number" dispensers like in a bakery and mounted it on the wall of the showroom. Then every once in a while he'd walk out of his office in the back, grab a number, and yell, "Number twenty-eight! Does anyone have number twenty-eight?" Customers didn't know how to react to that. Some of them would give him a puzzled look, others tried to ignore him, but some would sheepishly go over and take a number.

Ben loved that sort of thing, but the Bartons were all business, and after a while they started to clash.

For example, Ben sold a green Volvo wagon on European delivery to a family named the Hansons. In those days people could save a couple thousand dollars off the list price if they ordered a car in the States and then flew over and picked it up at the factory in Europe. They could drive around Europe on vacation and then drop it back off at the factory, and they in turn would ship it to the dealer that sold it.

Ben wrote the Hansons up, filled out the order form, the insurance form, and the shipping forms, and they gave him a five hundred dollar deposit. In cash. He finished the deal up after the office was closed, so he wrote them a receipt and pocketed the money, intending to turn it in the next morning.

To celebrate the sale, after work he started buying rounds at O'Brien's, and he used some of the deposit money to cover his tab. Ben and Mary Alice were still married then, and when he got home late smelling like beer, she got after him.

"Where have you been?" she snapped. "And what were you doing? No good, I'm sure of that!"

"Shows you what you know," he said. "I had a drink with a customer who owed me some money!" And with that he threw what was left of the deposit money at her. The next day he realized he had to make up the money, so he hit me up for a loan. Said he wanted to buy Mary Alice something for her birthday. If he'd have just told me the truth I'd have covered him, but Mary Alice and I were like oil and water, and I wasn't about to help him do something nice for her.

Ben never did come up with the five hundred dollar deposit, and when the Hansons came in and gave him a check for the balance, he stuck it in his top desk drawer and forgot about it. A couple months later I got a phone call from Lars Linblad at the Volvo Factory in Gothenburg telling me that someone named Hanson was there claiming that he ordered a car from us but they didn't have any record of it. I told him I didn't have any record of it either, but when Lars said that the salesman's name was Ben, I told him I'd call him back. I marched into Ben's office breathing fire, and he admitted what he'd done and gave me the Hansons' check, promising he'd make good on their cash deposit. Feeling like I had a little egg on my face, I called Lars back and said to give them a car. The only problem was, the Hansons had ordered green, and the only wagons they had at the factory with American equipment were turquoise.

"Give 'em a turquoise one," I said, "and tell them I'll have a green one for them when they get back to the States." I was sure we were going to have to eat the mileage and the shipping on the turquoise one, but somehow Ben had it sold before it landed on a boat in Baltimore. His commission on the wagon and a Mercedes coupe more than covered the five hundred, and Al told me to lighten up.

"Don't be so hard on the kid," he said. "No harm no foul, these things happen." They happened a lot to Ben, but he had a way of squirting out of trouble.

A few years later when Al remarried, he asked Ben to be his best man at the wedding, and that's when our friendship tailed off a bit. In Al's mind I'd dropped a peg or two; Ben had taken my place, and Al welcomed him home like the prodigal son.

Marriage agreed with Al. It took the edge off him. His wife, Kristen, was a good woman, and I think loving her mellowed him a bit.

Years later, when Al learned he was dying of cancer, we got together and wrestled with the whys of life. Kristen called me when Al was close to death, and I was holding his hand when he breathed his last breath. At his funeral I said that according to the Bible, "God doesn't judge by outward appearances but by the condition of our hearts" (see 1 Sam. 16:7). And that's how I knew Al was in heaven, because I knew his heart.

"Bet you're surprised to see me here," Al said.

"No," I replied, "not in the least. You were always more religious than you let on, soft and tenderhearted, like your mother."

"She said to say hi," he said, getting a little emotional. "And you could say that she's the reason I'm here. Now come on," Al insisted. "Let's take a ride. I think better when I'm driving." The tires spit gravel and dust as we exploded out of the driveway. It had been a while since I'd ridden in a car that's sole function was to go fast. We talked about the car, the old days, Ben, and the people we used to know for about a half hour, and then Al shifted the conversation away from small talk.

"Look," he said, "you and I were always pretty straight with each other, so I'm going to come right out with it. I always felt a little awkward talking about religion with you. It's not that I didn't believe in God, because I did. I just didn't like him very well, or to be more exact, I didn't like his brand of justice. You see, when I was eight years old, my dad died, and I prayed that God would do something. I believed in miracles, and each night I prayed for one, but God never delivered. One day after church I asked the preacher why, and he said, 'God has his reasons. He's always fair, and you must never question him. Besides,' the preacher said, 'he's not a pull toy on a string. He doesn't follow you, you must follow him.'

"I took that to mean that my father's death was somebody's fault, a payment of some kind, retribution for my sins, or my brother's sins, or God only knows what. The scales of God's justice had been balanced by my father's death. That may not have been what the preacher meant, but that's how I interpreted his words. After that, I never had much use for organized religion."

Al continued. "Evidently, it was also God's will for us to sell off most of the family farm and live hand-to-mouth. My mother worked her fingers to the bone, but each Sunday when they'd take a collection for the poor, she'd put a few pennies in the plate. The problem was, we were as poor as anybody I knew, but we never saw a dime of that collection money. So growing up, I learned two things: you can't trust preachers, and you can't trust God to do what you think is right.

"After that, I decided I'd better look out for myself. I spent my whole life trying to make enough money so that when we got older, Jane and I could enjoy life. But when I finally had the money, the one person I wanted to enjoy it with was gone.

> *God doesn't always answer our prayers as fast as we'd like.*

"For a few years there, I was so angry about it that I'd go over to that mausoleum, sit in the chair by the little brass plate that bore her name, and question God's fairness. 'Why Jane?' I'd ask. 'And why now, when we had so much to live for?' Why would a loving God take a mother from her children when they needed her most? Why would he take her from me when I needed her most? Was this my fault? Was God balancing his scales again?

"He didn't answer my prayers as fast as I wanted, so I answered them myself," Al said. "I came to the same conclusions I'd come to as a boy in Indiana: either God's not really there, or he doesn't care, or he and I had a very different understanding of what's fair.

"So now imagine how I felt when one day, out of the blue, you announce that you're going to pull a rich young ruler on me and sell everything you had to go and follow Jesus. Can you imagine how that made me feel? The God I was mad at was the same God you were going to give your life to. To be honest, I felt a little betrayed."

"I'm sorry, Al," I replied. "I never meant to hurt you."

"I know that. And there's no reason to be sorry. I was wrestling with some pretty dark stuff back then, and I'm the one who chose not to talk about it. When Satan is raising havoc in your life, you sometimes blame God. But now I have to talk about it, because I'm not the only one who's had those kinds of thoughts about God. Besides, in your line of work, you need to know what people are thinking."

> *When Satan is raising havoc in our lives, we sometimes blame God.*

We had pulled off the road into a pay-to-park lot somewhere in a big city. "I understand that I'm supposed to get you dinner," Al said. "I never was much of a cook, so I thought we'd get a pie."

I hadn't noticed until then, but as I looked around, it looked to me like we were in Chicago, a few blocks off Michigan Avenue, maybe on Rush Street.

Wherever we were, the streets were busy. People were moving along the sidewalk in swarms. Buses, bicycles, big cars and small ones wound their way through the city as taxi drivers honked their horns. Little boutique shops lined the streets, and a multitude of languages and music poured out into the street as we passed by. It was an eclectic symphony of sights and sounds.

"Where are we?" I asked.

"Jerusalem. The new one."

People were smiling at each other, laughter filled the air, and in the distance you could hear a street musician's jazz trumpet play "When the Saints Go Marching In."

"We're here," said Al, ducking in a doorway. The neon sign in the window said "Momma Lacarri's Pizza." Inside, the waiter in a crisp, white shirt and black bow tie showed us to a table.

Al ordered. "We'll have a deep dish with sausage, pepperoni, red peppers, and mushrooms. And bring us a couple of Cokes, please."

"How do you know what I want?" I asked.

"Trust me," he said, "you'll like it." And he was right. We talked about the old Chicago and the new Jerusalem and the excitement of the city, and during our conversation, Al ordered two slices of cheesecake for our dessert.

"I don't think I can eat another bite," I said.

"There's always room for cheesecake," Al replied. And somehow we managed to eat most of it.

We walked around the city for an hour or so, window-shopping, taking in the street entertainment, and buying a bag of caramel corn for the ride home.

As we started to drive out of the city, the sun was setting behind us, and the conversation turned again to the fairness of God.

"Listen," said Al. "What I didn't understand, and what you need to understand, is that the preacher was right, but it's a lot more complicated than that. Good and evil are sprinkled on every life like salt and pepper. We can't avoid it, and God doesn't always cause it. Sometimes it just is. Sometimes it's our fault—we bring things on ourselves. I don't like it, you don't like it, but it's a fact. There's evil in the world, but without the possibility of it, there'd be no possibility of you and me choosing good. The one comes with the other. Each of us is born with the potential for good and evil."

There's evil in the world, but without it there'd be no possibility of us choosing good.

"I get that," I said. When I was working at the state prison in Easton, I saw more evil than I ever wanted to, but even the worst offenders had a spark of good. You'd see it when they talked about their mothers or their girlfriends or even God, but the good was always overshadowed by evil. And the thing I wanted to know was this: Was that always their fate, was it the hand they were dealt at birth, were they simply born bad, or did they have a choice?

Al went on. "Imagine for a moment that there are two dogs standing beside you, a white one on your right and a black one on your left. Each dog has an insatiable appetite. Each and every one of us is born with both of them. As pups, they played with us in our cribs, and as we grew, they grew. Never once, not even for a moment, have they ever left our side. They are fiercely loyal, and outside of heaven's gate, they'll be our faithful companions till death. But don't reach out to pet them, and don't expect them to fetch your slippers, because these dogs will never be domesticated.

Reading the Bible doesn't make you immune to temptation.

"Their names are Good and Evil, and sometimes it feels like we're a rubber chew toy and they're playing tug-of-war with us in their teeth. Each of us has felt their push and pull at some time in our lives, and most of us constantly drift back and forth between the two. Even Saint Paul struggled with it. 'The good I would I do not,' he said in Romans, 'but the evil that I would not, that is what I do.'

"Like I said, we've all been there, and we'll never totally control them, but we can control what they eat. Now pay attention, because this is important. Here's how it works: Feed the one and he'll grow strong; starve the other and he'll grow weak. The one we feed will always be bigger than the other, but we get to choose which one."

"Listen, Al," I said, "I know all about the ugly underbelly of evil. I've studied it in depth. It was even the subject of my thesis. I tried to integrate what the Bible says about good and evil and what psychologists know to be true about human behavior."

"When the stuff of God becomes an academic exercise"—Al held up a finger in warning—"you're in trouble. Reading the Bible doesn't make you immune to temptation, and when you start to think that it does, that's when you're most vulnerable.

"One of the most effective cards in the Fallen One's deck is self-righteousness. When he can get us to busy our lives with the rituals of religion, then we've unknowingly joined the conspiracy. When he can get us to think of prayer, or Bible study, or giving as things to do on the holiness checklist, he has us where he wants us. And it won't be long before we start to think that we're special, better than everyone else. And believe me, that's a problem. Pride has pushed more than one person away from heaven's gate. God wants us to infect the world with his kingdom and kindness, not isolate ourselves from it. In fact, isolation is another one of the Fallen One's favorite tools.

"If we had the time, I'd take you to the edge of the great abyss. There, we could stand on the edge and look across at hell itself. No one is allowed to go across, but we can look across, and what we'd see is the torment of isolation. Everyone there is locked away in eternal solitary confinement. They're separated from God, from the people they love, and from everything that matters. There is no laughter to drown out the constant wail of loneliness, no gentle breeze to cool the sweltering sun, no music to soothe the troubled soul, no flowers to sweeten the foul air, and no food to satisfy the hunger for what might have been. There is nothing there but a sea of shadowy faces drowning in the eternal darkness of regret.

"If people really knew what waits there, they'd avoid it at all costs, but they don't understand. Christians talk about heaven, but we're squeamish when it comes to hell. We've bought into the lie that such uncomfortable subjects must be avoided, or at least sugarcoated, in the name of evangelism. Like I said, the Fallen One is good at this game. The black dog may rest, but he never sleeps, and he's always hungry. I know this makes you uncomfortable, and it should. But remember, it happened to your friend, and it could happen to you too."

"My friend?" I said, somewhat surprised that Al knew what had happened. James Harper had been a very prominent figure in the psychiatric community and the Christian community. The day before his wife discovered his affair, he had been speaking at a conference for Christian broadcasters. Everything had been kept hush-hush. As far as I knew, no one but James, his wife Kathy, and I knew anything about it. He dropped out of the public eye, and the two of them were trying, with my help, to put the pieces of their marriage back together again.

"You know who I'm talking about," Al said. "He was your teacher, your confidant, someone you looked up to, respected, admired, even envied. Clearly, he was a tool in God's hand. Because of him, a lot of people have put their trust in Jesus. He soothed their worries, comforted their sorrows, taught them how to live godly lives, and extended God's grace when they didn't. Everyone who knew him would say that he was a good man, but secretly, in the kennel of his soul, he's been feeding the black dog.

Surprising as it might be, the world's natural drift is toward evil, not good.

"The Fallen One served his kibble one bit at a time, in an online chat room, as his computer screen dimly lit the darkness. And as he did, the black dog slowly grew. On the other side of the kennel, the white dog yelped out a warning, hoping that he'd be fed instead. But he was ignored. Like DL, and Sampson, and God only knows how many other good men, he fed his lust a little bit at a time. And each time he did, he told himself that he was still in control. He thought he could handle it, but of course, he couldn't. Typed words and temptations spilled into telephone calls, and eventually there was a clandestine rendezvous.

"That, of course, was later followed by guilt and pleas for grace, but the black dog was still hungry. There were more typed words, more telephone calls, and more submission to temptation. As it always does, infidelity led to deceit, but even that would not curb the black dog's appetite. His hunger was not satisfied until it erupted in scandal, disappointment, and shame. And the point I'm trying to make is that nobody wakes up and says to himself, 'I think I'm going to go out and ruin my life today.' But it happens."

Al continued. "You see, contrary to popular belief, the world is not inherently good. In fact, the opposite is true. The earth is the Fallen One's turf, and it has been for a very long time. Surprising as it might be, the world's natural drift is toward evil, not good, and theologians have been telling us that for years. Augustine called it original sin, Calvin coined the term total depravity, and in Galatians Paul said, 'The sinful nature desires what is contrary to the Spirit, and the Spirit what is contrary to the sinful nature. They are in conflict with each other.'

"What they're really saying is what I've been trying to tell you: humanity is all part of a corrupted gene pool. It's the poisoned fruit from Adam's tree. Left to our own devices, we'll persist in destructive behavior. We'll cheat on our taxes, we'll waste time at work, we'll lust after our co-workers, we'll snap at the people we love, and we'll question God's goodness and love. And every time we do, we feed that black dog, and the world gets a little darker. Like I said, life is all about choices. Some good, and some not so good, so be careful. Be careful what you choose to do."

We should try to infect the world with goodness whenever and wherever we can.

We pulled into the driveway, and Al put his hand on my shoulder. "That's what cancer taught me," he said. "And this is what I have for you: Sometimes things happen that we don't understand. When they do, we can shake our fist at God or we can lay the blame at Satan's door. Do the latter. Feed the white dog. Repay evil with good. Infect the world with goodness, whenever and wherever you can. In the end, that's what really matters."

He didn't say it, but I knew our conversation was over. I got out of the car and told him I missed him, and both of us got a little emotional. "Keep an eye on Ben," he said. "He needs you now more than ever. And remember, if you want grace, you've got to give it." Then he drove away.

communion

Wisdom is a sacred communion.

Victor Hugo

13

I woke up late the next morning. So late, in fact, that when I went downstairs, I found that I had missed breakfast.

"There is some Raisin Bran in the cupboard, and milk and fruit in the fridge," Ahbee said as he went out the back door. "I've got some things to do with Rae today, but Josh will be waiting for you out front whenever you're ready."

I ate a big bowl of cereal, some orange slices, and a banana, and after doing the dishes, I went out to find Josh.

"Late night?" Josh asked with a grin.

"Yeah, Al's an old friend, and we had a lot of catching up to do."

"He's here partly because of you."

"I don't think so," I replied. "He was always a good man. One of the most honest men I ever met."

"That's true, but for a while in his life, he almost gave up on us. And he might have done just that if it hadn't been for his mother's prayers and for you."

"I'm sure it had more to do with her prayers than my words."

"Who said anything about words? It was your life that impressed him—what you did and why. Character is hard to come by, and he saw it in you. Come," he said, motioning with his head. "Follow me. Let's walk and talk."

The two of us walked along the shore for about a mile and then cut up along a path that chased a small stream. Josh was silent. Finally I couldn't stand the silence any longer, so I asked him a question. I really did want to know the answer, but I also just wanted to hear the sound of his voice again. It was like hearing your mother whisper that she loved you as you sat rocking on her lap as a child, or hearing your dad say that he was proud of you. I couldn't get enough of it, and so I asked.

There is an emptiness in our souls without God.

"Josh, there's something that's always bothered me. It's about your prayer, the Lord's Prayer. I pray it every night before I go to sleep and sometimes during the day when I'm frightened, or confused, or uncertain what to say. But tell me, why did you choose the words?"

There was a long pause before he spoke. "When I said, 'Our Father which art in heaven,' it was simply a statement of fact. It's where Ahbee is. We wish it weren't so. We wish he were here with us, because when we aren't with him, we feel the void of his absence. There is an emptiness in our souls without him. As someone once said, 'We're all born with a God-sized hole in our hearts,' and I am no exception. When I chose to step into time, I also chose to become one of you in every way. That meant that even though spiritually the Father and I were still one, I could now know the pain of physically being separated from him."

Josh continued explaining. "It's the first thing I noticed when I slipped on robes of human flesh: present with the body, absent from the Lord. Of course, someday that will be turned upside down. But for now, it's one of the things every human has to deal with. You see, like Adam, we all long to walk with Ahbee in the garden in the cool of the day. There are questions we'd like to ask, words of encouragement we'd like to hear, a certain comfort that comes from knowing he's close. Prayer is a poor substitute for his presence, but for now it's the best we have, and I simply chose to acknowledge the pain of his absence every time I talked with him. I could have said, 'I love you, I miss you, I'm incomplete without you,' but I chose to state it matter-of-factly instead.

"The other thing I wanted you to understand is that Ahbee is not just *my* Father, he's *our* Father, and he always wants what is best for each of his children. I know that's hard to understand sometimes. Particularly when he refuses to give you everything you want or when he imposes guidelines and limits on your life. But believe me, his law was not meant to restrict you but to protect you. It's what fathers do.

"The same could be said for 'Hallowed be thy name.' He is holy, separate, different than anything on earth. To put it simply, he is holy, and humanity is not. So as close as I might have been with people, I would still always be separate and different. Does that make sense to you?"

"Yes," I replied. "I think so. I can't experience it, but maybe I can understand it."

"Exactly," said Josh. "And when I said, 'Thy kingdom come, thy will be done,' I was expressing a hope of what might be, what should be, and what could be. You see, the *coming* and the *doing* were initiated by God, but it's continued by you, and each time it happens the conspiracy collapses a little. I wanted you to know that no matter how much danger you might be in, if you're doing his will and bringing about his kingdom, you are also safe in his arms. I also wanted the world to have a taste of what you've had these last few days—the absence of pain and evil, a sense of safety and purpose, and the confidence that only comes from being comfortable in your own skin.

"In God's kingdom there is no jealousy, no envy, and no coveting your neighbor's wife, his life, or anything else he might have. There is unimaginable contentment whenever the kingdom comes. Everything and everyone realizes that they are loved by the Creator and that they were created with a purpose. That has always been the will of God, but humanity squandered the gift away for an apple in Eden.

"Think about it. A salmon doesn't secretly wish to be a northern pike. An oak tree has no aspirations to become a maple. A beetle doesn't break into a butterfly's house in the middle of the night and try to steal its colorful wings. There is a sense of contentment in the animal kingdom that humanity can never know. The hippopotamus waddles down to the river each night to take his bath and says to himself, 'What could be better than this?' The shark glides through the waters of the deep and thinks, 'What more could anyone ever ask for?' The giraffe nibbles the sweet leaves at the very tops of the trees and says, 'Surely, no one has a better life than I.' Only humans lay awake at night plotting how they might take what belongs to someone else.

In God's kingdom, everyone realizes that they are created for a purpose.

"That's why I taught you to pray for *his* kingdom and *his* will to be reestablished once again. When it happens, then there will be no need to pray for anything else. It will be like finding an enormous treasure buried right under your nose, like discovering a pearl of great price."

Then Josh said, "Let me ask you a question. Do you remember the Beatitudes?"

"Yes," I replied. "Blessed are the poor, the peacemakers, the persecuted, and the pure of heart, as well as the meek, the merciful, and those who mourn."

"But now," said Josh, "did you ever stop to think that short of the kingdom coming, the only way any of them will ever be blessed is if the church does it? You see, I came to usher in the kingdom, but it was just a beginning. Unless those who come after me continue what I started, the kingdom will be nothing more than conversation until I come again."

Josh shook his head slowly, and after a long sigh, he continued talking. "People are forever asking, 'What would Jesus do?' instead of simply going out and doing it. I don't want this to sound as harsh as it's going to, but what the church needs is less talk and more action."

Part of me wanted to ask, "What about all the food drives, and the clothes and medical supplies that are donated, and the mission trips?" But I knew all too well that what we do is a trifling compared to what we could do. He was right. We talk a better game than we play.

> *People are forever asking, "What would Jesus do?" instead of just doing it.*

As a little boy, my mother taught me to give a dime for every dollar I earned, and growing up, I thought that was what everybody did. I was shocked to hear that over 80 percent of the people who claim to follow Christ give significantly less than that. Once I was sitting in a committee meeting, and an elder of the church said that he wasn't happy with the way things were going, so he'd decided to give only a dollar a week. A dollar!

What was even worse was that he'd get up at our quarterly congregational meetings and spout off about how we spent the money we collected. He was well respected in the community and he talked a good game of Christianity, so I'm sure most people thought he was a generous giver and had every right to voice his opinion. The problem was, I knew better, and it ate away at my soul.

> *Statistically, 20 percent of the people give 80 percent of the money.*

Finally, before one of our meetings, I caught up with him in the hallway and told him that if he complained, I was personally going to give back his fifty-two dollars and tell him to sit down. He turned red as a tomato, but he never said a word.

After that, I always wished someone would start the church of the tither. If you don't give, you can't come. Of course, no one ever did. I guess it just sounds too un-Christian. Forgetting that he knows our every thought, I was surprised when Josh responded to mine. "It's un-Christian to expect any less," Josh said with a smile, and I knew he was right.

Suddenly I realized that we had walked our way back to the cottage, and there in the driveway was Carol's Volkswagen.

"What's up with that?" I asked.

"You're going home after supper," Josh said, and a profound sadness welled up in my spirit.

"So soon?" I asked. "But there's still so much I want to ask you. I have so many questions."

"No one ever gets all their questions answered," he said. "That would take an eternity; in fact, that's what eternity is all about. For now, you must learn to live with uncertainty. Life is about trusting that Ahbee has the answers even when you do not. Can you do that, Scout?"

Whether we know it or not, we're all homesick for heaven.

"I can try."

"That's all we ask," Josh replied. "That's all we've ever asked. Now before we go inside, there's one more thing I wanted to talk to you about," Josh said. "And really, it's the reason we wanted you to come."

We sat down on the back steps. For a moment neither of us said a word. Then, after a heavy sigh, Josh tilted his head slightly and said, "Sky, what I need to talk to you about is the Christian conspiracy."

"I wondered when we'd get around to that," I said. "Whenever it came up, I'd hear little bits and pieces, and then you'd quickly change the subject. It's about time somebody tells me what's really going on with all this."

"You know more than you think," he said, "and to be honest, at times you've been a part of it."

"How can I be a part of it when I don't even know what it is?"

"Simple," Josh answered. "You've helped perpetuate the myth that Christianity is about a moment of conversion, a solitary act of commitment, a time when you give up your old life and give your heart to Ahbee."

"Isn't it?"

"That's part of it, but that's like saying that running a marathon is about buying a pair of running shoes. That's just the beginning. There's years of training, sacrifice, and endurance, and then there's the race itself to be run. And yes, those who finish well will be rewarded. Everyone who dedicates their life to making my kingdom come, on earth as it is in heaven, will get heaven thrown in.

"But the idea that Christianity is only about getting to heaven is at the core of the conspiracy. The Fallen One wants you to believe that it's about escaping from this world and getting to the next. But Christianity isn't about escaping the world—it's about changing it.

Your job is not to bring people on earth to heaven; your job is to bring heaven to the people on earth.

"He wants you to believe that this is a transaction, that it's like putting a check in the box, that you can just give your heart to Ahbee one minute and then go back to business as usual the next. But when you truly give your heart to Ahbee, you'll never be able to go back to business as usual again. Instead you'll be about your Father's business. Does that make sense to you? Are you getting this down? You need to get out ahead of the rest on this one, Scout. I'm counting on you to show them the way."

I looked down, a little ashamed to look Josh in the eye, and sensing my discomfort, he paused for a few moments as I tried to absorb the weight of his words. Then, as I lifted my eyes and looked into his, he smiled and continued. "As a Christian your job is not to bring people on earth to heaven. That is my job. That's what the cross is all about. Your job is to bring heaven to the people on earth. To feed the hungry, to clothe the naked, to care for the sick and the crying and the dying. When you do that, people will start asking, 'Why? What's your motivation? What possible reason would you have for making that kind of a sacrifice for me?' And when they start asking questions like that, then sharing your faith will be easy, then lives will be changed. It's simple, really. Do that, and you'll change the world. Don't do that, and nothing will change. Like I said before, *what you've done to the least of these, you've done to me.*"

When I silently nodded my head in agreement, Josh said, "Let's go inside."

As we walked into the dining room, I realized that this would be our last supper, and more than that, I also realized that this was the meal I'd really come for. The table was set with crisp white linens, fine china, elegant crystal, beautiful flowers, and an odd assortment of flatware. I was about to ask Josh about the hodgepodge of forks and knives, but then suddenly the room began to fill up with people. One by one, every chair was taken. Everyone I'd shared a meal with that week came and took their place at the table: Mom, Herb and Gerry, Grandma Great Kate—everyone was there. The room rumbled with conversation and laughter, and Mom patted the empty chair next to her as if to say, "Come, sit here by me." So I did. Just like I would have at home.

Like everyone else I knew, I'd always had this hunger in my soul for something I could never satisfy. And what I'd come to realize was that this was it: the communion of the saints. What I was really homesick for all these years was heaven.

Ahbee and Rae sat at the head of the table, and Josh took the empty seat between them. As he did, what had been impossible to understand before, now made perfect sense. The mystery of God was acted out in front of me, and for the first time in my life I began to really appreciate the oneness and the harmony of the three. It dawned on me that I'd never talked to all three at the same time, and suddenly I wondered why. Why do I pray to one and not three? When I say my nightly prayers or when I want something tangible, I pray to the Father. Other times, when I want inspiration or wisdom, I pray to be filled with the Holy Spirit. And when I need someone to listen and encourage me, it is Jesus every time. As I saw their uniqueness and oneness more clearly, I promised myself that my prayers would be different in the future—more personal, more listening and less talking.

It was for me that they nailed Jesus to that tree.

I was brought back to the moment when Michael came in from the kitchen with a large silver tray and placed it in front of Ahbee, Josh, and Rae. As a hush fell over the room, Josh took a large loaf of bread and broke it, while Rae poured us each a glass of sweet red wine. For a moment we all sat frozen in silence, and then Ahbee began to speak.

"Eat," he said. "And as you do, join with us in the pain and sacrifice of love."

The bread was bitter and dry, impossible to swallow. I looked across at the scars on Josh's hands and tears slid down my cheeks. I could not escape the thought that it was for me that they nailed him to that tree. Finally, overcome with the agony of it, I whispered what was on my heart.

"It isn't fair," I said. "It just isn't fair."

"It isn't fair," said Ahbee. "It is love!"

Then he raised his glass, smiled at me, and said, "Come. Come and taste the sweet taste of forgiveness."

We emptied our glasses, and one by one, the people I had loved and lost said their good-byes. In the end, only Ahbee, Josh, Rae, and I remained.

Josh walked up to me, cupped my face in his hands, and said, "Remember what I told you, Scout. You must learn to see the world as I do. And when you do, you'll see that it's full of broken, frightened, hungry, and uncertain people. Some of them need healing. Some of them need holding. Some of them are hungry. Some of them are heartbroken. And all of them need saving from something, even if it's from themselves. What they need are not more words or theories but more love.

"If you want to follow me, it will cost you. You must be willing to give up a part of who you are for their sake—a part of your time, your money, and most of all, a part of yourself. When you do that, then the blind will see, the deaf will hear, and the fallen will rise up and walk in the way of Ahbee once more.

"When you see the world like I do, you'll know that sometimes it's people that need changing, and sometimes it's conditions that need changing, and more often than not, it's both. But wherever change comes, the kingdom comes as well."

With that he smiled, gave me a bear hug, and slowly walked away.

Next Ahbee stepped forward and spoke. "I want you to have this," he said, handing me the fork I'd used for dinner. As I looked more closely at his gift, I realized that it was part of my grandmother's silver set.

"Is this—" I began to ask.

"It is," Ahbee answered. "You brought it with you in your lunch in second grade at Woodcliff School, and you left it in the lunchroom. Do you remember?"

"Yes, I remember. My mom was upset that I lost one of Grandma's sterling silver forks."

"Well, now what was lost is found, and I want you to keep it as a reminder. Remember going to your grandma's house when you were a boy?" Ahbee asked me.

I nodded.

"Do you remember what she used to say at the end of the meal? As the dishes were being cleared from the table, she'd say—"

"Keep your fork," I interrupted. "She'd say, 'Keep your fork!'"

"That's right! And what she meant was that something better was coming: cream pie, apple pie, cherry pie, something wonderful. And this is your reminder of the same thing. This is just a taste of heaven, something to tide you over, but keep your fork because something better is coming."

Then we embraced, and Ahbee walked away.

Only Rae and I remained now. I looked across at her, hoping for some direction for what to do next. Sensing this, Rae said, "I'll walk you out."

With that, we went out through the kitchen and into the driveway.

"You're leaving me too?" I asked.

"No, you can't get rid of me so easily! I am always with you. At times I've been your guardian, your guide, and even your guilty conscience. Never once, not even for a moment, have I ever left your side, nor will I. You may not see me, but in your heart you'll know I am there. But it's getting late, and you've got a drive ahead of you. You'd best be on your way."

As I got in the car, Rae climbed into the seat beside me and said, "You might want to check the mail on your way out."

I started the car, pulled out of the driveway, and drove down along the lake road. As we went through the back gate, Michael was standing guard. "I'll leave the gate unlatched for you, Scout," he said as we drove by.

As I looked at him in the rearview mirror, I saw my reflection as well. I was older again. The gray had returned to my temples, and laugh lines creased my cheeks. I could see the sun setting in the distance. Streaks of orange and yellow splashed atop the ripples of the water, and the low rumble of thunder welled in the southwest.

I took Rae's advice and looked inside the mailbox with my name on it. There I found an envelope addressed to me, and inside was a note from Ahbee.

"My son," it said, "there are things you need to learn, and things you need to teach. Let me begin with the learning. This life is the preschool for eternity. Much of what you want to know is simply beyond your ability to understand. You must take baby steps. Grasp what you can understand, grapple with what you can't, but don't let it eat you up inside. Wisdom takes time. Don't be in such a hurry. All your questions have answers, but you're not ready for all of them. That's what eternity is all about.

"When you were a child, many foods were simply too harsh, too sharp, too complex for your young palate to appreciate. If you stroll down the baby food aisle at the supermarket, you'll find strained carrots, peas, and applesauce, but you won't find things like onions or chili peppers, garlic or salsa, or mustard, or even salt. These things come with time. You need time to develop a taste and appreciation for them. If someone tried to feed them to you before you were ready, you would make a face and spit them out. It's not that it would be bad, it's just that you wouldn't be ready for them yet. And that's the way it is with life.

"Many of the things that shock you or that you find offensive now will one day prove to be the spice of life. They are the very things that molded your character, deepened your faith, challenged your thinking, and softened your heart. Think about it. Have you been closer to me and the people who matter in your life in the easy times or the hard times?

"You have done well in preschool. You have learned many things, but there is so much more to learn. So don't shrink from such things or pull back and make a face. Accept them for what they are. Embrace them. Live the salty life. Remember, as Josh has told you, 'You are the salt of the earth.'

"And then, as for the teaching," the letter said, "start with the inner circles. There is a natural progression to these sorts of things. When Josh sent out the disciples, they were to go from

Jerusalem, to Judea, to Samaria, to the ends of the earth, and your Jerusalem is Europa Motors."

I knew what he meant. I had to start by talking to Ben. It wasn't going to be easy, but it was necessary. There is an old Dutch proverb that says, "If everyone swept off their own front porch, the whole world would be clean," and I had some housecleaning to do.

"You must teach," Ahbee wrote, "with the same patience, gentleness, and grace with which you've been taught."

I looked over at Rae, who smiled and raised her eyebrows inquisitively. "Do you understand what the letter means?" she asked.

I nodded and said, "I understand some of it."

"Some is enough to start," she replied, and then ever so slowly, she began to fade from my sight. "Even though you don't see me," she whispered, "I can still see you," and in my heart I knew it was true. The ancient promise echoed in my memory: "I will never leave you nor forsake you" (Heb. 13:5 ESV). It was and is a comforting thought.

I was alone, but I didn't feel alone. Now more than ever before, I felt like God was with me, and there was something comforting about knowing that Rae was watching over me. I crossed the bridge that spanned the creek and started to head south toward the highway. As I drove along, shadows chased the tree line, rain clouds filled the western sky, and gradually the light was swallowed up by darkness. I began to hear the raindrops dance against the windshield like the sound of a leaky faucet, and as I turned on the wipers, I realized that I had come full circle.

I was torn between going home to the ones I love and going home to the ones I'd left behind. For a few minutes I thought about turning around, but I didn't. I went home thinking that I'd keep my thoughts to myself. I wanted what had happened to have its effect on me before I tried to explain it.

As I drove back home my mind was reeling. I knew I had some things to do, but I didn't know where to start. Unbeknownst to me, that had already been taken care of. As I pulled in the driveway I saw Dad's white Jeep Grand Cherokee Limited sitting there. I knew it was his because he has a "Support Our Troops" ribbon on the tailgate and I could see his fishing gear through the window in the back.

Besides, Dad had driven the same make, model, and color car for the past twenty years. He'd buy a new one every couple of years or so, but it was always a white Grand Cherokee with tan leather. Dad used to say, "It's nobody else's business how often I get a new car, and this way nobody knows except me and your mother." If the truth were told, I think the only reason Mom knew that Dad was driving a new car was that, for the first few weeks at least, it didn't smell like a bait store in the back. Unlike me, Dad didn't fall in love with cars. He saw them as a tool, a way to get from point A to point B, and because he liked to be able to fish in places that were off the beaten path, the Jeep was the perfect car for him.

As I pulled in the driveway, Dad got out of his car and started walking toward me with a deliberate and determined look on his face. Before I could say a word, he started talking.

"I know what's going on, Sky, and I'm sorry. Ben told me all about it, and I want you to know this is my fault. I favored him. I made it easy for him. I apologized and made excuses for him his whole life. I gave him a pass. I let him say things and do things that I never would have let you say or do because I was reliving my life through him."

"Wait, Dad—"

"That's part of the problem," he said. "I've waited too long already. Your mother warned me, but I wouldn't listen. I wanted him to do what I couldn't. I always regretted not playing pro ball, not finding out how good I really was. When I had my shot with the White Sox I thought I could make it. That scout and my coach both said I had all the moves, I was a natural, it was a gift from God. So he gave me a train ticket to Chicago and at the tryouts I was a machine. I hit everything their best pitcher threw at me, and afterwards the coach said, 'Kid, go in the locker room and tell Red I said he should get you a locker and a uniform.'

"That's when I told him that I'd love to be on the team but I had one problem: I promised my mother I wouldn't play ball on Sunday. 'I'll play every game on every day but Sunday,' I said, 'and I don't even care if you dock my pay some for sitting it out on the Sabbath.'

"'Listen, kid,' he said. 'This is your shot. Think about this before you answer. Think about seeing your picture on a baseball card. You've got talent. You could maybe be somebody in this league. But if you don't play on Sunday, you won't play at all.'

"My heart sank. I wanted to play bad, real bad, but I'd promised my mother. 'Well,' I said, 'I'm real sorry to hear that, but I promised, so I guess I'll just have to take that train ticket home.' Inside I was hoping he'd change his mind. I was hoping I was good enough to make an exception to the rule, but evidently I wasn't.

"'You don't play, we don't pay,' he said, and he turned and walked away. Brokenhearted, I hitchhiked my way back home with a lump in my throat and a pocket full of regrets. Since then, I've always felt God sort of let me down that day in Chicago. I always figured he could have softened that coach's heart. He could have made him give me a chance, but he didn't. Then Ben came along, and I thought God was making it up to me. The kid was a natural, a genuine ball player. Football, basketball, baseball—he took to sports like he was born to play, and so I treated him like he was special. The problem was, when he couldn't play ball anymore, he didn't know who he was anymore. He couldn't figure it out, and I couldn't help him, so you had to."

"Look, Dad," I said as we walked through the garage and into the house, "I never minded helping. I knew that you were as devastated as he was about that, and it was my turn to step up. I just did what I could do, that's all."

Dad slumped into a big leather chair in the living room and spoke softly. "The only problem was that when I stopped treating him special, you started treating him special. You gave him a job, you looked out for him, you looked the other way, and you bailed him out when he messed up. And don't you even try to deny it because he's already told me all about it.

"He came to me and asked for his inheritance early. And what could I do? I'm his father and I'm your father, and to hear that you two were at odds with each other broke my heart. It was my fault and it was mine to fix, so I sold a piece of property I had to cover the prodigal's debt. He and I went down to the bank and paid off the note yesterday."

"Property?" I said. "What property?"

"Remember that cottage we used to rent when you were a kid?" he asked, and I nodded that I did. "Well," he said, "there was this piece of property down the road from there called Promise Point. Your uncle Herb and I used to go bass fishing off the rocks by the bay, and one July I caught a five-pounder. I was telling your mother about it later that night and she wanted to see it, so the two of us drove over there just before sundown. We sat on a picnic table underneath a couple of white pines, and we started talking about you kids and how much you loved it up there, and then she noticed a For Sale sign hidden in the weeds. She took out her lipstick and wrote down the number on an old bulletin in her purse, and I told her I'd check it out. 'Do you promise?' she said. 'I promise,' I said, and then I carved the words and our initials into the top of that old picnic table. I said, 'This place is a little taste of heaven, and someday we'll build a house up here.'

"We never did, but I did check into it. The lot was listed by a place called Paradise Reality, and when I called them they said they'd sell it to me on a land contract. I made monthly payments on it for the longest time, but by the time I got it paid off, life had changed. First there was Ben's accident, then Sharon and Jim moved out of town, after that you went back to school, so I sat on it. Then, right after Ben came over and told me about what was going on, a guy named Michael DeAngelo from Paradise Reality called me out of the blue and told me he had a buyer for the property if I'd be willing to sell it.

"I can't explain it, and you probably wouldn't understand if I tried, but it just seemed like a God thing to me, so yesterday I signed the papers, got the check, and Ben and I went down to see Jake at Old State and made things right. I told Ben that when I die that money gets deducted off the top of his share of my estate, and I expect you to make it happen, okay?"

"Okay," I said. "I'll see to it, but I hope I don't have to do anything about it very soon."

"None of us can know that," Dad said, "but I do know that I'm eighty-nine, and I'm ready."

"Well, I'm not," I said. "I want you to stick around for a while."

"I know, I know," he said. "But I wanted to make this right. And I also wanted to tell you how sorry I am for what I said the night of the accident. I never should have done that, but I needed to unload on someone. I thought you could take it, but I realize now how much pain my words caused. The truth is, in the things that count, you're the strong one, and you always have been. In that way you're the one who's most like me, because when times get rough, everybody leans on you. I should say this more, but, well, you know how it is. Son, I'm proud of you."

By this time both of us were starting to get a little emotional. "It's true," he said, "and you know it's true!" After a long, awkward moment of silence, he gave me a hug and silently walked out the door. I wanted to yell, "Dad, wait, there's something I've got to tell you," but he looked over his shoulder and said, "I'm going over to your sister's for supper, and I'm already late. If you want to come I'm sure you're welcome, but Ben asked me to tell you that he'd be out in the barn if you wanted to talk."

The barn was a four-stall pole barn nestled in the pines behind Dad's house. He used it as a workshop and a place to store his boat. I used it as a place to rebuild cars when I was younger. Most nights Ben would come out and help, or at least try to. Once in a while Dad would come too, but most nights it was just Ben and me.

We'd spend hours twisting wrenches and tinkering with things, and we'd get into deep discussions about everything from girls to God. Around ten we'd often end the night by going down to Vitale's for a pizza. We both enjoyed those nights in the barn, and at some point out there we went from brothers to best friends. In the past few years we'd sort of put that part of our lives on the shelf, and I'm sure that was part of the reason that we'd grown apart. Ben was still my brother, but the relationship was heavier now. It was something we both had to work at.

As I drove out to the barn, I regretted letting things between the two of us get the way they were, and I wondered if inviting me out here was Ben's way of inviting me back into his life. I hoped so, and I let my mind play with what might be, but as always with Ben, I really didn't know what to expect.

The barn was about a quarter of a mile down a little two-track back through the pines, and when I turned into the clearing, I felt like I was stepping back in time. The barn was wrapped in turquoise and white ribbed steel siding that was rusted and weathered. It had two windows in front, each of which was propped open with a stick, and one of them still had a cracked pane in it from a baseball that got away from me when I was about eight. Weeds had grown up around the cement slab by the front entrance, and the horns off a nine-point buck were mounted above the door.

There was a gunmetal gray 2002 BMW Z3 parked out front,

and I knew from the dealer plate that it was Ben's. He liked to drive hot cars, and this one sizzled. It was the mirror image of the one Pierce Brosnan drove in the Bond movie *GoldenEye*, and the car sparkled in the late afternoon sun.

On the east end of the building, the old single-stall wooden garage door was partially rolled up. As I ducked underneath it and walked inside, it was like seeing an old friend. The barn was dimly lit by four fluorescent lights that hung off chains that dropped from the ceiling. The floor was cracked, yellowed concrete that sloped to a drain in stalls number two and three. Oil and paint had been spilled and sprayed on it over the years, and it kind of had the appearance of a speckled bass.

In the first stall Dad's weathered old fourteen-foot Starcraft sat on the trailer. It had a flat tire, but the boat looked pretty shipshape. The fifteen-horse Evinrude was tilted up on the stern ready for travel. The poles, cushions, and life jackets were stowed neatly in the side bins. The oars were fixed in the locks and tucked inside the fins on the back, and the chain link anchor dangled off the bow. There was a small dent in the starboard side of the hull from when I ran her into the dock one night coming in from bluegill fishing. As I looked at it, I thought, *It's been too long since I've taken Dad out fishing.*

In the next stall was a scuffed-up old Honda 90 motorcycle we used to run up and down the two-track when we were younger. Like the boat trailer, it had a flat tire, plus the brake handle was bent, the mustard yellow paint had faded, and the seat was torn and tattered. An open can of Quaker State sat on top, and by my guess it had probably been there for five years or more. Propped up against the side of the cycle was a faded piece of blue plastic with the letters *VW* on it. It had been part of a Volkswagen lollypop sign we'd had in the car business. Ben said that he wanted to frame it and hang it up at the car lot, but by the looks of it he never got around to it. Next to the Honda was the Lawn-Boy we used to cut down the weeds around the barn and a fire engine–red

Radio Flyer wagon with wood rails. Inside the Flyer were a pair of garden gloves, a little trowel, and a three-tined weeder that Mom used to use in her garden.

In stall number three a Coleman lantern, a blue hand-crank ice auger, and Sharon's purple Schwinn Stingray bike hung from hooks in the ceiling. Dad's old workbench stood up against the wall behind them. The top of the bench was made out of a piece of salvaged bowling alley, and he'd made the legs out of four-by-fours. On one end there was a vise bolted on the top and on the other end was an anvil. To say the bench was sturdy was an understatement. On the wall behind the bench there was a four-by-eight piece of pegboard with tools outlined and labeled in Dad's block-style capital letters. A calendar from the forties with a picture of Betty Grable on it hung from a hook. She was in a bathing suit with her hair stacked up on top of her head, looking back over her shoulder and smiling, and Dad said he put it up there because it reminded him of Mom when she was younger. By a row of screwdrivers on the other end of the bench he'd tacked Mom's high school graduation picture, and when I saw it I thought, *If only he could see her now.*

It was in this stall, where an old Volvo now sat covered in dust, that I rebuilt the motor of the first car I ever owned, a black Triumph TR2 with two white racing strips that ran across the hood and trunk. I bought it from a guy who'd raced it, and when I got it, it had the number three piston sticking out of the side of the block. Piece by piece I took the front end off the car, sequentially numbering each piece with masking tape labels as I went. Dad came out and saw the parts scattered around the barn floor and bet me a hundred dollars that I'd never get it running again. He'd have won the bet if Herby hadn't come to my rescue. Herb came over every night after supper for three weeks and helped me put it back together with a used short block I'd gotten from the junkyard.

For a time I was lost in the nostalgia of the place and wondering why I'd kept my distance from Ben and the barn. Then without warning he came sliding out from underneath the old Volvo that was parked in stall number three. It was a dark khaki–colored 1962 544 with red-ribbed leatherette interior. The design of the car was totally retro, and it looked like a '46 Ford coupe that shrunk when it got caught in the dryer. Ben looked up at me from the creeper and said, "Hey bro, Dad called and said you might drop by. I'm glad you did. You know more about these old ones than I do, and I could use some help."

He told me that he'd taken the vintage Volvo in on trade from a guy who'd had it parked in his grandfather's garage since 1973. He said it ran when he drove it in there but it didn't start now. Ben confessed that he probably put too much money into the car but had fallen in love with it. It reminded him of an old ice racer we use to have, and I said that I agreed.

"These things are built like a tank," he said, "and that little fourbanger tractor engine will run forever." He was hoping to restore it for Easy and said he thought it would make a great high school graduation present for him. "Can you imagine being on campus your freshman year driving a chick magnet like this old Volvo?"

"I don't think Easy is going to have any trouble attracting girls," I said, but I had to admit it would make a sweet ride. "You could trick it out with chrome wheels and custom paint."

"I'm thinking about maybe keeping it original," he said, "but first I've got to get it running. I put in some fresh gas, got a new set of plugs and points sitting on the bench, and I'm charging the battery, but when I tried turning it over earlier I don't think it was getting any gas. I'll bet it's got something to do with those Zenith-Stromberg carbs. They always were a little touchy. You want to take a look?"

"Sure," I said, "but you might have to have Dave come over if you really want it done right. I was always better at dolling them up than tuning them up."

"I've got complete confidence in you, bro," he said. "I'm going to slide under here and finish putting new oil and fuel filters on this thing, and while I do, why don't you tackle the electrical stuff?"

"Sounds like a plan," I said as he slid back out of sight.

A half hour later he crawled back out, grabbed the keys off the bench, and slid awkwardly behind the steering wheel. I could tell his leg was bothering him, but before I could ask about it he said, "You feather the butterfly on those carbs, and I'll try to breathe a little fire in this beast."

It took a little coaxing, but after a few misfires and some sputtering, the old Volvo was humming like a sewing machine. Ben hollered in delight as he revved it a few times and then shut it down. Then he ran around to the front of the car where I was standing and swallowed me up in a big bear hug.

"You and I always did make a great team," he said, still holding me close, and almost whispered the words, "Whatever happened to that?"

It was a rhetorical question. We both knew what happened. The accident and its aftermath had driven a wedge between us.

"I know it won't be easy," Ben said, "but I think we've got to talk about this. At least I know I've got to talk about it. This is the elephant in the room every time we get together as a family, and I'm sick of dancing around it. You know as well as I do that it's been eating us both up, and it's got to stop."

"I've been talking to Pastor Bill," he continued as he let me go and looked me in the eye. "He's been helping me see things a little clearer. He said that if I'm going to really give my life to Jesus, then I've got to give him all of it, and that includes the stuff between us. Then last week as he was about to break the bread he said that communion was a feast of forgiveness, and that the opposite was just as true. Unforgiveness is a meal in itself. We feed off our anger, and our resentment, and our disappointment, and the more we taste it the more we want. Before you know it we're licking our lips imagining the sweet taste of revenge. The problem is that rather than satisfy our hunger, it eats us up inside, and when the meal is over, bitterness and guilt have picked the meat off the bones of our souls. And that's where I've been for too long.

"I know the accident wasn't your fault, and I also know how much I let you and Dad down in all this. Oh, you tried to hide it, but you couldn't. You guys are both lousy liars, and that night in the hospital it was all over your face. Everyone knew that I was never going to be what I could have been, and I couldn't deal with it. I was horsing around. I was showing off for the girls on the beach, and I lost my footing. I slipped.

"It wasn't your fault. It was an accident, but at the time it was easier to blame you than it was to accept the blame myself, so that's what I did. Then after that, anytime anything else happened, I just kept blaming you. In my mind all of my problems were your fault. If you hadn't brought that boat up there that day, if you hadn't turned when you did, if you would have done something different, then everything would be different now. Believe me, I threw myself quite a pity party at your expense, and you wore my guilt like an overcoat.

"My whole life, whenever I fell down or messed up, you were always there to catch me, or to cover for me, or to make things all right, and this time you weren't. So right there in that hospital room I started blaming you. I decided that you owed me. You were going to have to pay, and I was going to see to it. Blaming you became my crutch."

"It's all right, Ben," I said. "You had good reason to be mad, and hey, the truth is, I've always blamed myself for that day too."

"I know you have," Ben said, "and that's just wrong. The only thing more wrong was me letting you do it. I should have stepped up and taken this like a man, like you would have done if things were the other way around. But I didn't. Maybe it's too late, maybe you can't forgive me for what I did, but I hope you can because I can't live with the guilt anymore."

"It's all right—" I said again, but Ben interrupted me.

"No, it's not all right," he said, "and you saying it isn't going to make it so. I've got to clear the air about this, and you've got to let me. I feel bad enough that Dad had to step in and bail me out with the bank, but I've got to do this with you. So let me finish talking, okay?"

"Okay," I said.

"Here it is, Sky," he continued. "My whole life I've looked up to you. In fact, I wanted to be you. Whatever you did, I did. It was like I was your shadow, but I always knew that I was never quite good enough. When we were kids you were always bigger, always stronger, always smarter, and you always knew just what to say. You were like Dad, only younger. Everyone knew that he was so proud of you, and I wanted that. I envied that.

"The only place I got that kind of respect from him was on the athletic field. When I played baseball, or football, or basketball, Dad noticed. Athletics was the one thing I could do better than you. Hey, you said it, Dad said it, everybody said it: 'You're a natural!' It came easy to me. I loved sports, and I loved the attention I got even more.

"All I ever really wanted to do was to make Dad proud of me, and football was my ticket. For the first time in my life, I was the favorite. I was the one he talked about to his friends, and I liked it. But then that day in the hospital everything changed. I looked in his face and all I saw was disappointment, and it hurt. It hurt big time, and I'm only now starting to come to grips with that.

"Looking back, even then I knew this was my fault. The problem was, I wasn't ready to face it. I needed to hide from it for a little while. There was a side of me that didn't want to blame you, but there was also a side of me that did. So for a while those two sides waged a war inside my soul, until finally the darker side won out.

"You were my crutch, and I've been limping through life ever since. You know it's true and I do too. Ever since then we've had this chasm, this unresolved anger between us, and it just keeps popping up over and over again. It's like that Whac-A-Mole game down at the arcade. We push it down and it pops up somewhere else.

"I guess what I'm asking is, do you think there's any way that you can forgive me, Sky? I know it's a lot to ask, and I also know that it's going to take some time, but the only way I could see for this to get better was for me to come clean and to tell you how sorry I am. I didn't mean to drop all this on you at once, but once I got started it was kind of hard to stop. I guess what I'm really trying to say is that I want my brother back."

By now Ben and I were both crying. Tears chased down his cheeks and mine, and then he said again, "I'm sorry, man, I'm so sorry," and with that his voice trailed off into an uneasy silence.

I knew it was my turn to talk, and I didn't want to leave him hanging there, but the problem was, I didn't know where to start.

"Ben," I said softly, "I really don't know what to say. Of course I forgive you. I had no idea that you felt this way. Listen, like you said, it was an accident. And as for you letting me down, if anything the opposite is true. I think I let you down. If anybody needs to apologize, I think it's me. This was more my fault than yours.

"I was trying to look like a big wheel to you and your friends. I wanted you guys to think I was cool, so I drove up in a Mercedes dragging that MasterCraft. I never should have brought that boat up there in the first place. Dad was right. You guys were elite athletes. You were in training. You had your whole life ahead of you. You should have been focusing on football, not girls and water-skiing. And yes, I knew you blamed me for some of this, but I blamed myself more. So thanks for having the guts to be so honest, Ben. You have no idea how much hearing you say that has lifted a burden off my back. But if we're making confessions, then it ought to go both ways. I've got a few things to say too.

"The truth is that I rather enjoyed the role of rescuer. It inflated my ego. Every time you called needing my help, I'd slip into a phone booth, put on my cape and costume, and rush right over to save the day, like Superman, and if someone noticed, so much the better. Every time I'd hear someone say, 'You've sure been so good to your little brother, you gave him a job, you set him up in business, you're always there for him, he's lucky to have a brother like you,' my head would swell a little more. If I was your crutch, you were my cross.

"I had a little bit of a messiah complex going. I could play the martyr as long as someone was there to notice. Metaphorically at least, I'd drag you through the streets on my back, looking as brave and as Christlike as I could. And if anybody asked, I was always ready to tell the story. 'My poor misguided brother messed up again,' I'd say, throwing you under the bus, hoping that someone would nominate me for sainthood.

"If we're going to be honest about all this, then I've got my own apologizing to do too. This little game of ours was a two-way street, my brother, and like you, I played my part with a certain amount of willingness."

"So what you're saying is that if I can find a way to look past your black heart, maybe we can be brothers again?" Ben said with a grin.

"Yes," I said. "At least that's a place to start."

"Well then," Ben said, "why don't we start by working on this old Volvo and see where it takes us?"

"I'm in. That sounds like a plan to me."

"Since you're feeling so guilty," Ben added, "why don't we run down to Vitale's and you can buy us a pizza? Then we can come back here and get back to work on Easy's car."

"What makes you so sure that's the kind of car Easy's going to want?"

Looking over at the 544, Ben said, "What's not to like? It's simple, it's reliable, it's good-looking. If he takes care of it that thing will last forever. In fact, I'll bet that's the kind of car they drive in heaven!"

"Not exactly," I said.

"What do you mean by that?"

"Let's go get that pizza and I'll explain it to you."

Somewhere in our conversation that night, Ben and I started to be brothers again, and the next day when Carol and the girls got home from Chicago, I told them about our talk.

"Your mother would be so happy," Carol said. "It's what she wanted more than anything else."

"I know," I said. "Believe me, I know. What mattered most to her was family, and knowing that some of us were struggling with each other broke her heart."

We talked for about a half hour, the girls showed me some of the things they bought in Chicago, and then after the girls went home Carol said, "I thought you were going to go up north to check out that cottage?"

"I did," I said. "It's a long story. Why don't we make some lunch and go out on the deck, and I'll tell you all about it."

At first I was hesitant to tell the story. I hemmed and hawed around for a while, hoping not to have to tell her everything, but no matter how hard I tried, little by little, she pulled the story out of me. "There's something eating at you," she said. "I can tell. You don't have to talk about it right now if you don't want to, but I want you to know that when you're ready to talk, I'm ready to listen."

I nodded my head in agreement and held my tongue for the next couple days. Then that Friday we took a long drive together, and little by little I told her what happened. Of course she believed it, because she believes in me. The same thing was true of the girls. Dad and Sharon wanted to believe, but it was a little more of a struggle for them.

"If you say it happened," Dad said, "I'll believe you, but you know, sometimes dreams can seem pretty real."

"It wasn't a dream, Dad," I said.

For another couple of weeks there was a tug-of-war going on in my heart, but then one night Ben and I were out in the barn working on Easy's 544 and he tipped me over.

"You've got to tell the story," he said. "You can't keep something like this to yourself; it wouldn't be right. Whether you want to tell it or not really doesn't matter. God wants this story told, and he gave it to you to tell."

That was three years ago now. Since then Ben and I are more open and more honest with each other than we've ever been. We're both better people because of it. Iron sharpens iron. So reluctantly, cautiously, with his encouragement, I've even written some of the story down, and doing that has had a profound effect on me. It may not change the world, but it's certainly changing me.

Nowadays I work at spending less time on the things that don't matter and more time with the people who do. Evidently, it's more noticeable than I thought. People tell me that there's something different about me, that some kind of change has taken place, a subtle shift in my attitude and values, and all I can say to them is that visiting heaven will do that.

I'm not saying that I've got it all figured out—I don't. I still struggle with things like hunger, poverty, injustice, violence, natural disasters, and of course death, but life doesn't seem as random as it once did. I have hope. I know God, and I know he's working things out in ways that I might not understand. So when I don't have all the answers, I can put my trust in the One who does. At least I try to, but honestly, I'm still a work in progress. Roz was right: God's not done with me yet.

But I've been given a gift. I was sent ahead to scout the way.

I've had the chance to peek over the horizon and see the great beyond. I've tiptoed up to the line between life and death and caught a glimpse of the unknowable mystery. I know with absolute certainty that the best is yet to come. So even if you're not quite convinced about my story, keep your fork! Something better is coming.

the benediction

Each Sunday I close our church service with words that express my hope for anyone who hears them. I want to let them serve as a benediction for my readers as well.

May God's seeking comfort find you.

May his loving arms bind you.

May his might protect you

And his wisdom direct you.

And may the joyous love of Jesus Christ

Be with you and those you love

Now and forevermore. Amen.

Dann A. Stouten is senior pastor of Community Reformed Church in Zeeland, Michigan, one of the fastest-growing churches on the West Michigan lakeshore. After a highly successful career in the auto industry, Dann returned to school and earned his DMin in narrative preaching. This is his first novel.